SING CAROLS
WITH
THE ANGELS

SING CAROLS
WITH
THE ANGELS

•

MARY LEASK

An Avalon Romantic Mystery

AVALON BOOKS
THOMAS BOUREGY AND COMPANY, INC.
401 LAFAYETTE STREET
NEW YORK, NEW YORK 10003

PRINTED IN THE UNITED STATES OF AMERICA
ON ACID-FREE PAPER
BY HADDON CRAFTSMEN, SCRANTON, PENNSYLVANIA

This book is dedicated to the many friends and family who kindly and patiently read, reread, encouraged, and criticized my writing.

Lynn hurried into her hospital room to gloat over the empty bed beside hers. What a piece of luck! The person to come down from Intensive Care had developed a slight temperature and was to be held there until the next day, so she would be able to hold the interview in her room rather than in the tiny public waiting room at the end of the floor. Carefully, she looked the room over estimating its strengths and weaknesses. The walls were a quiet blue, probably to calm the patient, she mused, while the vinyl armchairs and cotton thermal blanket on each bed were a soft, hopeful yellow. A picture of a vase of daffodils repeated the color. On a bed table was a jar containing flowers that a volunteer had made a habit of keeping full from the remnants of flowers left behind by discharged patients. This kind act had done much to cheer

1

Lynn over the past three weeks since she, herself, had come down from Intensive Care.

Deciding on a plan of action, she started to move the chairs so that they made a small interview space between the two beds. Standing back in the doorway, she imagined the meeting with the economist, a cousin of one of her doctors. She had forgotten to ask, but she expected that he was an older gentleman since he needed clerical assistance. A younger man would have used a word processor.

The chairs were not set to her liking. They had to be just right. So much hung on the success of this interview. She had to control the event so that the economist would be so impressed with their meeting that he would overlook the obvious disadvantages, such as the fact that she had a leg in a walking cast and was using a cane, and that her nose and cheeks were crisscrossed with tape and bandages. To make matters worse, her jaw had been wired and consequently she mumbled when she spoke. However, none of these things interfered with her ability to use a word processor.

She turned the chairs so that they angled toward each other, pulled the portable hospital table to the end of the bed, and placed copies of *The Financial Post, Saturday Night* and *Maclean's* on it. Standing back, she studied the whole effect. The magazine seemed too obvious so she opened *The Financial Post* to an article on the effect of Mexico entering the North American free trade zone. This topic had been discussed on television constantly so that she had found the piece easy to understand. Maybe he would have read it, too.

Glancing down at her watch, a Timex that had survived the accident along with her handbag, she saw that it was nearly time. Going into the bathroom, she combed her newly cut hair over the scars that ran along the hairline on the right side of her face. She tidied the blue track suit that a volunteer had acquired for her with cash found in her purse. Taking a big breath to calm herself, she went back into the room.

Now that she was ready she had nothing to do, so she picked up *The Financial Post* and, standing before the table, looked for another article to read. She was to recall later that she had felt his presence even before he spoke, and had started to turn, when he said, ''Ms. MacDougall? Ms. Lynn MacDougall?''

The man before her was no aging economist! Instead of the stooped, elderly gentleman she had imagined, she found herself looking at a tall, loose-limbed man in his early thirties dressed in beige cotton pants and a bomber jacket over a casual white sport shirt. Instead of the aging eyes and heavy spectacles she had expected, alert gray eyes watched her from under a wide brow. A well-formed nose and jaw and generous mouth completed the face of one of the most attractive men she had ever seen. Almost-blond hair waved across his forehead and looked fair against his golden-tanned skin. This was her economist?

As she gaped at him, she saw a look of horror appear on his face. ''What in heaven's name did you let my cousin do to you?'' he demanded.

It was going to be worse than she feared. Standing as tall as her five foot four inches allowed, she answered his question. ''If you mean the fact that your cousin repaired my jaw so it is as good as it was before the accident, then, that is what I let him do. The bandages you see were placed there by a plastic surgeon four days ago, and I understand that when they come off, I will be better than new. Neither will keep me from typing your work, Dr. Stone. Please come and sit down.'' And she indicated a chair near her bed table. As he headed for it, and actually sat down, she continued, determined to control the interview. ''Tell me how I can help you with your work.''

As she sat down, she could tell from his expression that he did not like the way she had set the pace. So she folded her hands on her lap and looked, she hoped, expectant.

He fidgeted for a moment, looked around the room, eyed the magazines, obviously trying to think of some graceful way to get out of the situation without hurting her feelings. However, she had no intention of letting this happen. She had to get out of the hospital. She needed a safe place to stay, and this man's house seemed perfect. When he still did not reply, she raised her eyebrow and prompted, ''I understand that you are writing a book.''

He seemed to realize that he was outmaneuvered for the moment, and with a sigh, answered her question. ''Yes. I have almost all the research material sorted out and need someone to organize it on the word processor. Then, I will begin the actual writing. There are also statistics to be entered and reference material to be looked up.'' She was sure that he added that last bit hoping that she would not know how to get the information.

She may have lost her memory of herself before the

accident, but she had not lost her skills. "If you have a modem and a telephone, then I am sure that I can get the material you want."

She knew by the annoyed look on his face that she had him cornered. But the glitter in those gray eyes told her that he had not given in. He reached down for a laptop computer he had placed beside his chair, stood, and took it over to the movable table. Opening it, he turned it on and pulled some papers from his inside jacket pocket. Placing them on the table, he turned to her. "Would you care to demonstrate your skills?"

He stood back, his hands in his trouser pockets, while she got up and with the aid of her cane, made her way to the table. She wished she had had a chance to become more adept at walking with the cane, but she had no intention of letting him know. She took the first paper, straightened it out, and then began to enter the material. As she worked, a wave of astonishment washed over her. She was somehow familiar with this material. Every technical word! She had to control the trembling of her hands as she worked. This was the first glimpse she had had into her forgotten past. Taking slow breaths to ease the racing of her heart, she finished the passage and passed the machine to him. As he read the entry, she tried to place the information in some context, but none came.

Silently, he scanned the entry and found it correct. Wordlessly, he handed her back the machine. She took the second sheet. It was covered with handwriting. Again, she entered the material without error, and handed it to him. He studied it, and then looked at her with narrowed eyes. "Is it correct?" she asked.

He grunted an affirmative and looked around. His eye fell on the copy of *The Financial Post* she had been trying to read and picked it up. "What did you think of this article?"

She chuckled to herself at his last-ditch effort to untangle himself from the situation. Taking it from him, she explained, "I did not read more than the first paragraph when you came in, however, I did read the article before it about the consequences of the Mexicans entering the North American free trade zone. Would you like to ask me some questions?"

He had the good grace to blush at that, and turn away. She watched him as he walked over to the window and looked down. Finally, he turned and asked, "How soon can you begin?"

She knew this was his last attempt to get out of hiring her, and she had her answer ready. "Tomorrow."

Looking startled, he echoed, "Tomorrow?"

"I have no need to stay in the hospital taking a valuable bed anymore. The bandages on my face, the cast on my leg and the wires on my jaw can all be removed in the doctor's office or in the Out-Patient Department. I assumed that Dr. Dunlop explained that to you when he recommended me."

"No, he did not," he said grimly, and took another turn around the space at the end of the beds. He sure was one handsome man, she thought as she watched him come to terms with the fact that she had won. He turned to her abruptly. "Are you sure that you are well enough to work for long periods of time? After all, the advantage of having you live in is that you can be at my beck and call at all hours.'' When she raised her eyebrow at this one, he added, ''Within reason.''

Deciding that it was time to take a stand, she stepped around the table toward him. ''Dr. Stone, I am simply bored out of my skull here. I'm anxious to have something constructive to do. The fact you can provide a place for me to stay while I work will give me a chance to recover from my injuries in some kind of privacy. Your cousin would not have suggested me if he had not been sure that I was competent and physically able to fulfill your requirements. I promise you that next Thursday the bandages will be removed from my face, so you'll no longer feel as if you are looking at Frankenstein's bride!''

That embarrassed him because she had hit the nail on the head. He had not been able to get past the bruising and the bandages on her face. With a shrug of his shoulders, he gave in. Packing up the laptop, he said, ''So be it. What time will you arrive tomorrow?''

Being careful not to show her relief, she explained, ''Discharge time is about eleven o'clock. I'll take a taxi to your home. Dr. Dunlop says it isn't far. I should be able to start work after lunch tomorrow afternoon.''

Adam Stone was furious, so furious that he skipped the elevator and ran down the hospital stairs two at a time. But the exercise did nothing to ease his temper. Blast his cousin's tender heart. Didn't he understand the pressure he was under? Now he not only had to worry about the book, he had to worry about the girl. How could he expect her to stay up at all hours to accommodate his crazy writing habits? It did not matter that he would be supplying her with a suite in the house or providing the services of a housekeeper. He knew he would find it impossible to drive her the way he drove himself.

Why hadn't he just said he didn't think the arrangement would work? The answer was all too evident. There was no way he could refuse those violet eyes. He had seen determination and desperation in them. For some reason unknown to him, she was frantic to get this job. Pausing as he reached the ground floor, he reflected that there had to be more to this situation than he had been told. Cousin Tom had been too secretive about it. He had not warned him that this young woman would be so battered. Instead he had mumbled something about an accident, but had assured him that she was competent. And to be honest, a small voice reminded him, she was competent. But she was so frail, so devastated, that he could not imagine that she would be anything but a burden.

As he walked through the ground-floor hall and exited to the parking lot, he had to admit that he admired her. She had anticipated every move of his, and beat him at every turn. He could almost hear her say "checkmate" when she had finished the samples perfectly and then offered to discuss the article in *The Financial Post*. He could not remember when he had been quite so efficiently outmaneuvered. He supposed his dear cousin was sitting at home, rubbing his hands together with glee and waiting for a call from him to confirm that he had manipulated him into hiring his protégée. Well, he would not give him the satisfaction. Tom would just have to wait and hear the news from his patient tomorrow.

*   *   *

That night, Lynn had another of the nightmares that had haunted her since she had regained consciousness, only this nightmare was clearer and more terrifying. This time the sense of suffocation and confinement was clearer, more specific. She could remember the coarse texture of a heavy cover that seemed to press down on her face, and she felt the sharp pain of restraint as she struggled to free herself—something she never succeeded in doing. She always woke before she could figure out what was holding her hands and feet so painfully behind her back.

Lynn lay back on her hospital bed and tried to will her heart to ease its frantic pace but the images refused to fade. There was no doubt now that this dream was built on something beside fantasy. Her subconscious was dredging up flashes of an incident that she was sure had happened. After all, she had the proof on her wrists and ankles—fine, red-lined scars that still stood up in welts. She remembered how the medical staff and even a policeman had questioned her carefully about them following her recovery from the coma. But she had not been able to tell them anything that would explain how she had gotten them. In the end, they had chosen to ignore their presence.

There was more that she had hidden from the hospital staff and the police. She could remember nothing about herself before waking in the hospital. She had no knowledge of Lynn MacDougall, did not remember any detail of her life in Ottawa, or any other part of it. And yet, she could remember this dream in such detail, and her general knowledge was still intact.

By the time her badly battered face had healed enough for her to speak, the dreams had started, and caution had made her decide that it would be unwise to draw attention to her lost memory. After all, there had been enough information in her handbag to establish who she was to everyone's satisfaction. She was Lynn MacDougall, aged twenty-three, born in the province of Nova Scotia, but, it seemed, a person on the move. She had been employed in Nova Scotia and Quebec, and more recently, worked in Ottawa for a civil servant at the Economic Council of Canada. It appeared that she had just left her job to move on to Toronto and new experiences. All this she had learned from the police and medical staff.

She had done well in covering up her handicap. Only one doctor had come to know the full truth about her loss of memory. He had been the maxillofacial surgeon who had reconstructed her jaw. He had been at her side when she came out of the coma, and had taken a special interest in her case ever since. He had been astute enough to figure that she was suffering from more than post-trauma amnesia. When she realized he knew, she decided to take him into her confidence. She explained about her dreams and scars, and begged that he let the matter rest. She feared if the news got around that a real amnesiac was in the hospital, the media would become involved and her whereabouts announced to one and all. It took some convincing, but finally the doctor agreed to keep silent until she felt she had fully recovered from her injuries. It had been the same doctor who had arranged for her to see Adam Stone. She suspected that he felt less guilty about keeping her secret by knowing where she was so that he could keep an eye on her. They had both agreed that it would be wiser not to tell the economist about her memory loss.

Her relief at getting the job with Adam Stone must have relaxed her subconscious enough for her to recall her nightmare more clearly. Its frightening detail made her more grateful she had someplace to go where she could hide, for she was sure that someone had meant to harm her seriously, and possibly still intended to do so.

She was going to have to be very careful. She knew that Adam Stone did not want her and was pretty sure that he would snatch at any opportunity to get rid of her. She had to make herself indispensable. Secondly, she was going to have to keep well out of his way when she was not working, for she was sure that he was astute enough to figure out that she could not remember her past. Turning over on her side, she willed herself to sleep with the desperate thought that if she was not rested she would made a bad impression.

It was a vivid September day that contributed to the magic of Adam Stone's house. The air had lost its summer mugginess, and in the clear, crisp atmosphere, everything shone. The trees were awash with sunlight, and here and there, an early flash of red or orange announced the coming of autumn. Lynn was surprised when the taxi entered a very exclusive section of Toronto. Even then, she was not ready for the uniqueness of the house in which she was to live.

The taxi turned into a curved drive, and there, as if it had been transported from the rocky wilderness that covered parts of Ontario a hundred miles north of Toronto, was a house made of pink granite. Its modern planes and angles glistened in the sun. Cleverly planted about it were trees of that region—pine and cedar, maple and oak, birch and sumac. As she was helped out of the car by the driver, she was stopped by a sense of familiarity. The smell of the pine needles and the heat from the sun on the sparkling rock struck an emotional echo in her heart. Here was a secure place, a fortress of rock where she would be safe. She was not sure why she felt this way. She just knew that the granite and pines signified safety. Even as she stood, enchanted by the house, the front door opened and a smiling, dark-haired woman in her late thirties greeted her. "You must be Miss MacDougall. I am Adam's housekeeper. Please come in."

With a smile, she led Lynn through an elegant entrance, then through what appeared to be a formal living room. Off-white walls and light carpets set off chesterfields and chairs of blue and ocher arranged before a magnificent pink granite fireplace. Above the mantel, she was startled to recognize a painting by Lauren Harris. The walls were alive with the color of other paintings she recognized. Until that moment, she had not known that she knew anything about art or artists.

The housekeeper led her into a lovely large room that combined a sitting area and entertainment center along with a sleeping area and washroom. This was a room that had obviously been lived in. The chair and chaise longue set before the center were well worn, and the style of the bedroom furniture suggested an earlier decade. The room itself was decorated in light beiges with pastel chintz chairs and bedspread. Sheer curtains let in the light through large windows. Lynn found herself quite shaken at the thought that this lovely space was to be hers.

The housekeeper smiled at her and said, ''By the way, I didn't introduce myself. I'm Philomena Sousa. I'm here each day to prepare your meals, and generally keep the place tidy. There's another woman who comes in once a week to do heavy cleaning, and a gardener who works on the grounds. Adam's hard at work, and asked me to see that you're settled in. Unfortunately, I have a dentist's appointment later, so Adam will see to your lunch. When you are ready, come through the living room and down the hall to the kitchen.'' She looked at Lynn's bag, and then when she realized that she had nothing but a plastic shopping bag and her handbag, looked puzzled.

Embarrassed, Lynn explained that she had lost all her belongings in the accident. Everything she owned was in the plastic shopping bag. It contained basic necessities and another track suit. She would, she explained, go shopping for more clothes when she had her bandages removed from her face and had earned her first pay.

When the door closed behind the housekeeper, Lynn relaxed for the first time that day. *From one safe house to another,* she thought. Now where had that idea come from, she wondered.

Looking further, Lynn found a series of spacious closets waiting for her clothes. Next to the closets was a bathroom walled with the palest of pink Italian tiles, and possessing every convenience: a shower, Jacuzzi bathtub, a set of elegant, white tile sinks with gold taps, the latest of toilets, and to her amusement, even a bidet. A cupboard contained numerous sets of soft, pink towels and a selection of expensive lotions and soaps.

Lynn leaned against the bathroom door and pondered her good fortune. It seemed incredible that she should end up in such luxury after the events of the past weeks. In fact, it was almost frightening. Why had she been selected to be the recipient of such bounty? She who had so little claim to it. She who knew so little of herself, or of the violence that seemed to be part of her past. Well, she thought, the least I can do is earn this. And she promised herself then, standing in the beautiful bathroom, that she would do her best for Dr. Stone and Dr. Dunlop, and she would accept responsibility for any situation that arose from the return of her memory.

Hastily, Lynn freshened up and then, with as much speed as possible, found the kitchen. Leaning against the door frame, she paused to catch her breath and calm herself. The kitchen was a surprise. It was as if the owners were compensating for the muted walls and floors of the other rooms. The cupboards were a pale-yellow limed oak, and walls and floor a warm creamy-white. Placed about the room was an abundance of greenery: hanging, spreading and flowering. Off the kitchen was a charming breakfast room into which the sun poured. Standing in front of a coffee machine that was gurgling noisily was her employer, unaware of her approach.

She studied him for a moment. His crown of fair hair set off his strongly boned face, however, there were still signs of tension around his eyes and mouth as if he had been driving himself too hard. He was long and lean of body, and she wondered if he was a jogger. Today, he wore a pale-blue sport shirt, open at the neck, with sleeves turned up to the elbows, and light-brown jeans of some brushed fabric that stressed the length of his legs. He moved with efficiency and a vibrant energy as he poured the coffee, and then turned to see her standing at the door.

With a smile that eased the lines of tension, he brought two coffees over to a counter that had stools on either side. *He also has a megawatt smile,* she thought.

''I othought that it might be easier for you to sit on a stool for now, but if a chair would be better we can go into the breakfast room.'' She assured him that the stool was fine. He returned to the counter where he picked up two other mugs. ''I figured you might be hungry so I heated up some soup. Out of a can,'' he grinned. ''Tom warned me that you were on a special diet. Here's a curved straw. There are more in the cupboard at the end of the counter. I also bought a list of liquid and soft foods that Tom said you could eat. I left them in that cupboard for now so that they are easy for you to reach. If you need anything else, let me know.''

Lynn was quite overwhelmed. Was this the same man who had been trying to avoid hiring her? ''Thanks,'' she smiled. ''I really am hungry. This is the first time I have been outside the hospital since the accident and I think I must've used up a lot of nervous energy.'' Then, because she felt shy, she continued, ''This is a lovely house.''

''It is lovely,'' he agreed. ''It belongs to a friend, Ian Browning, a retired president of one of the Canadian banks. His wife, Marion, had a stroke two years ago. That was when he put the addition on containing your suite, the solarium and study, and an exercise center. When his wife recovered from her stroke, he decided to take her on a leisurely trip around the world. He knew that I was returning to Canada and suggested that I stay here. He felt the house would be safer with someone in it.''

She began to sip her soup through the straw. It was difficult to do this with any degree of poise as the soup was thick enough to cause slurping sounds. After one or two attempts, she could not resist grinning at him. ''It's a terrible temptation to blow bubbles.'' He laughed at that, and she relaxed.

As she finished her soup and began her coffee, Adam explained, ''You met Philomena. She is the Brownings' housekeeper and a treasure. She is a widow with two sons in high school. I know that you will like her. She is clever, conscientious, and a pleasant addition to the household. The only rooms she is not allowed to clean are the ones in which I work.''

Now would be a good time to discuss the job, she thought, so she asked, ''Tell me about your book, Dr. Stone.''

He looked at her for a moment. He's got gray eyes with warm rays of yellow in them, she noticed. Then he nodded his agreement, and began. ''Tom probably explained that I am an economist with considerable experience at the international level. In fact, I have spent a lot of time with the European Economic Council, and have also consulted throughout the world. There has been so much happening to the world's economy, so many shifts in power, and so much increased debt that I felt there was a need to present an analysis of these changes. In my arrogance, I thought I had the answers. That was until I started to organize and write my ideas down. Now, I feel like I have a monkey by the tail. It's all very interesting, of course, but also takes all my energy. That's where you come in. I have been writing down my ideas by hand, and to my dismay, I find myself buried in a mountain of notes.''

At this point, Lynn was interested to see a rather uneasy expression cross his face. Wishing to reassure him, she said, ''I didn't find your handwriting that bad.''

With a wry grimace and rubbing the back of his neck, he admitted, ''It isn't the handwriting that is the problem.'' And getting off the stool, he waited for her to stand, and led her to a door leading out of the kitchen, saying, ''There's no easy way to explain this.'' Then, with a shrug, ''Oh, well, you'll see.''

Lynn was fascinated. Adam Stone was embarrassed. Slashes of color touched his cheeks. Whatever is he about to show me? she wondered. He opened the door into a solarium. Wonderful cedar arches ran up the wall and across the ceiling, framing large windows that looked out onto the lawn and gardens beyond, so that her first impression was that somehow the out-of-doors had come inside. Her next reaction was one of complete amazement, for before her, literally on every surface of the room, the sills, the casual green-print furniture and the carpeted floor, were piles of paper. And then she understood. This was what Adam was embarrassed about. This was his book! No wonder he was having trouble.

Lynn was overcome with a desire to laugh. In fact,

she could feel a chuckle start to form, but she glanced up at him and squashed the urge. He was looking at her defensively, waiting for a response. Working hard to keep a straight face, she said, "Maybe you would like to explain to me how your...er...system works."

That immediately brought a suspicious glance but she managed a look of innocence, and he turned back to the piles. "I thought that you could enter the material in each of these piles of paper onto the word processor. Actually, the piles are organized in related groups." When he caught a look of disbelief flash across her face, he grinned. "It's true. I'll show you how later."

Then he turned with some pride toward what appeared to be a new desk and computer in the left-hand corner of the room. "I purchased this for you, and I'll get anything else you need. Just make a list."

Curious, she asked him, "Do you use a computer?"

"Not really. I've always had secretaries. I have enough trouble with a laptop computer. In fact, I bought the thing, but rarely use it. I type as if I have two left thumbs. I never have been able to find the time to develop the skill."

Great, she thought. "Did you get an instruction book with this computer? I think this is a much fancier machine that I have used before. It will take me a while to familiarize myself with it and the word-processing program. Actually, if it's all right with you, I'll just settle down and figure it out. When I have everything organized, then I think it would be a good time for you to explain your...system."

For a moment, she thought he was going to disagree, but she misjudged him. "Are you sure you feel up to starting today? Tom warned me you would probably be tired at first, and that I should let you set your own pace.''

Dear Dr. Dunlop, she thought, he certainly had anticipated her every need. But she assured Adam she really was anxious to get started. Looking around, she asked, ''Where is your desk?''

He turned and pointed to a doorway at the other end of the solarium. ''There's a study in there. Ian Browning had his books put in storage and I was able to set up my own books. Actually, it has been marvelous, getting all my books under one roof. I also have a large file of articles and reference material, and another very much neglected computer. I just use it for the modem. I also have a fax machine so the whole world is actually at my fingertips. In fact, if you think you are all right, I'll go back in there now.''

Relief swept over her, and she assured him that she was just fine. He paused as he was heading for the study door. ''Oh, by the way, I tend to get a bit absent-minded about time when I'm working. Just interrupt whenever you want to know something.'' And with those words he disappeared.

And now, she thought, let's hope that I remember everything one needs to know about a computer!

Four days later, Lynn stopped her work at the word processor, stood up and stretched. There was room to walk in part of the solarium now, and she moved toward the great glass windows to enjoy the view. This room with its wonderful cedar arches was her favorite. Whenever she got tired or tense, she would approach the windows and let the scene outside revive her.

The Brownings' property was wide and deep. A lush green lawn ran back to beds of autumn flowers and varied shrubs. Behind them stood what must have been the original woodlot that existed before the city's expansion. Oaks, maples and pines, basswood and walnut formed a formidable wall around the property. There were subtle signs of autumn now. Here and there a branch of maple glowed like a medieval torch against the greens of the other trees. Fat black squirrels dangled from the walnut trees and scurried about in the leaves while vivid blue jays gorged on acorns.

Ted, the gardener, was working away on the grounds. He had been kind enough to get out the summer furniture after Lynn discovered that the lawn's paths had been made of smooth bricks, ideal for walking with her cane. After that, she had walked the paths to exercise her leg. In the morning, when she took a break, she would go outside and Philomena would bring out a tray with coffee and sweet Portuguese confections that Lynn could soften in her coffee. She would sit under the umbrella and let the peace of the place ease her tensions, for she still had nightmares though never as bad as those in the hospital, and she still had moments when the loss of her self overwhelmed her with a dark blanket of despair.

But most of the time she managed. The work was challenging and interesting, and hauntingly familiar. Adam Stone left her alone, and judging by his air of abstraction and the steady stream of papers that were piled on her desk, he was working at a frantic pace. They occasionally lunched together and always shared supper. He was polite and preoccupied, and Lynn liked it that way.

With a sigh, Lynn turned toward her desk. She had felt so optimistic when she had arrived at the house, sure that she could face the world. In actual fact, she admitted to herself, she had used the granite-faced house as a refuge, a beautiful fortress that kept her safe inside and the rest of the world out, and she liked it that way, also.

The next day Lynn took a taxi to the plastic surgeon's office to have her bandages removed. As she rode there, she remembered the bizarre experience of having to select a nose that she could not remember from a series of sketches Dr. Mysinski had shown her since the only picture they had of her was the one on her driving license, and it was not particularly clear. It certainly gave no clue to the profile of her face.

Lynn had leafed through the pages, and come upon one she was sure was right. When the doctor asked if she was positive, she had nodded but could not have explained why she felt that way. Well, now, she thought with a churning of her stomach, she would know.

A nurse led her into an examining room where she waited. Finally she heard the doctor's voice outside the door. Panic washed over her, and her heart began a frantic tattoo. Yet she was hard-pressed to identify exactly what it was that she was afraid of, except that there had been such safety behind the bandages.

As if he sensed her state of mind, the surgeon quietly greeted her, calmly instructed her to sit on the side of the examining table, graciously helped her to do so, and asked the nurse for a pair of scissors. As he snipped and peeled away the bandages, he warned her that her face would be slightly swollen around her nose and cheekbones for at least another week.

When the surgeon asked the nurse for a mirror, her anxiety returned. With unsteady hands, she took the mirror. Summoning up all her courage, she lifted it and looked. The face in the mirror was quite unknown to her and a surge of such black, screaming disappointment swept over her that she nearly howled her despair. Somewhere in her heart of hearts, she had been counting on some miraculous alchemy that would render mind and face into her lost self. Instead, she saw only the eyes, brows and jaw with which she had become familiar, and an unknown nose.

A sound from the plastic surgeon made her glance up, and she realized that he and his nurse were waiting for her reaction. With trembling hands, she traced the bridge of her nose. In spite of the swelling, it was exquisite, perfectly balanced for her face, straight and wonderfully formed. Shyly, she smiled at the doctor. "You have made me quite lovely. How can I thank you?" His face relaxed, and his anxiety disappeared as she expressed her pleasure. He made a few notes in her file, and then said with a smile, "You can thank me by continuing to get better, and by avoiding any more highway pileups."

When Lynn left the doctor's office, she took the elevator to the ground floor of the medical building and stood in the lobby for a minute, not quite sure what to do next. With her uncovered face, she felt quite naked. There was nothing to hide behind anymore. Looking around frantically, she saw a coffee shop off the lobby, and hurried in and took a seat at a table. She ordered a soft drink and straw, and then fought the urge to get out a mirror and look at herself again. The ordinary action of drinking calmed her down, and she began to think more rationally. It occurred to her that it was possible she did not look exactly as she had before the accident. After all, she had only guessed at her profile, made her selection by instinct rather than knowledge.

Finishing her coffee, she hurried into the restaurant washroom. It was empty. Quickly she got out her driver's license and studied the picture. Then she looked at her face in the mirror. She really did not look much like the picture. The face in the driver's license was roughly the same shape, but in it, she had long hair and it seemed pulled back quite severely from her temples to hang straight over her shoulders. If her bandages had seemed like a mask behind which she could hide, maybe, by stressing her shorter hair, she could continue the disguise. Glancing at her watch, she saw that she had only been gone an hour. She had told Adam that she would take time to shop. Well, she would get her hair styled, too.

Leaving the medical building, she asked a taxi driver to take her to the shopping mall nearest to her address. When she arrived there, she paid the driver and headed for the hairdresser's. When the stylist was finished, she was delighted with the short cut that capped her head in soft waves.

Thanks to Adam's generosity, she had her week's salary a day early so she headed to the department stores next. Luck was with her and she found a fleece-lined ski jacket on sale that was light enough for the present but warm enough for winter. The jacket was made of patches of nylon—periwinkle, jade and fuch-

sia. Its colors set off her face and matched a new jade
track suit she had found. She was also lucky enough
to find a very expensive woolen skirt and silk blouse
on a discount floor. Paying for her purchases, she
changed into the new track suit and slipped on the
jacket. Looking in the mirror, she saw a colorfully
dressed stranger. So this was she—Lynn MacDougall.
Feeling much braver, she marched out of the stores
and headed home.

Adam just happened to be standing in the living
room when Lynn's taxi arrived. Who was he kidding?
He was there because he could not contain his curiosity. Hurrying to the door, he stepped out to the entrance and hastened to assist her. He was stunned by
the transformation before him. The young woman reminded him of some exotic bird, with her cap of shining black hair, green-clad body and jacket of brilliant
colors. She was quite beautiful. Even with the swelling, her complexion was camellia-perfect. As if suddenly conscious of his attention, she smiled at him
shyly, those glorious blue eyes questioning. He could
not help himself. He reached out and touched her face.
"You are quite lovely. Certainly never related to Dr.
Frankenstein."

He was fascinated to see her blush, as if she was
not used to compliments. The women he knew expected such remarks as their due. He had certainly
never seen one blush. Sensing her embarrassment, he
led her into the house, and watched her hurry to her
room.

*   *   *

Adam settled himself in the armchair in the solarium and stretched his long legs before him on a low
footstool. In the three weeks since Lynn's arrival, he
had made amazing progress. No longer did he feel
haunted by the ridiculous piles of paper. Instead, he
was able to immerse himself completely in his work.
For the last ten days or so, he had been able to take
the odd hour here and there away from the demands
of the study desk, and read in the pleasant surroundings of the solarium.

He liked taking a break in this room. Now that the
days were growing shorter, the autumn sun was lower
in the southern sky, and its beams slanted into the
room bathing everything with its warmth. It was not
just the sun that lured him out of his study. The presence of his serious young assistant also gave him
pleasure.

Her desk was on the other side of the room, slightly
angled away from him so that he only saw her partial
profile, but that was enough. Her face had healed completely. All signs of bruising and swelling had disappeared. The sun flooded over her now, igniting the
blue lights in her hair, and adding a glow to her delicate complexion. The only things to mar her loveli-
ness were dark smudges under her eyes, and he
wondered what stresses or pain caused those shadows.
Today, she was wearing a fuchsia track suit, his favorite, as its V-neck revealed the elegant line of her
neck and throat. As if sensing his attention, she turned
and smiled.

With a sigh, Adam returned to work. Lynn-
watching was not going to get his work done! This
time he concentrated for over an hour until a move-

ment on the other side of the room made him look up.
She was standing now, reading through one of the remaining piles of paper. In spite of the cast, or maybe
because of it, she moved with a gracefulness he had
never observed in another woman. It was something
to do with her posture and the swing of her hips. He
found it quite enchanting. But then, he thought, she
was a very intriguing woman, full of contradictions
and mysteries, and he loved the challenge of solving
a mystery.

For example, at that very moment she was doing
something he had neither asked her to do nor shown
her how to do. She was just starting a new pile of
papers, and was sorting them into logical subgroups
before she began to enter them into the computer. She
had only started to do this recently, and so far, he had
said nothing about it. Another recent activity of hers
had been the reading of books in his study. She had
been quite open about this. Did he mind if she read
some of his books? He had been amused at first. After
all, a typist would hardly be able to understand a
heavy tome on economic theory. But she had surprised
him with the book she selected—a very general text
on the top shelf left over from when he had lectured
first-year economics students during the time he
worked on his doctorate. After that, he had been
amazed to see a steady stream of books, each of in-
creasing difficulty, disappear with her each day when
she finished work.

And that was another thing. She worked like one
possessed. When he expressed his concern, she had
gritted out through that wired jaw of hers that she
hated to be idle and was enjoying every minute. With

a shrug, he had left her alone. However, he did keep an eye on her activities, and noted that she paced herself, taking a break to walk in the garden or going to her room for a short rest.

In spite of the fact that she completely ignored him except when they were working on a shared task or eating a meal together, he was learning about her. For example, she could be quite bossy, and had a well-hidden sense of mischief. Within a few days of starting to work, she had him buying filing cabinets for her, and then had him trained to indicate on his latest scraps of paper, by number, which topic they belonged to, and then to put the paper in a tray where she would deal with it.

They had had quite a battle of wills over this, and she had explained, as if to a child, that all he had to do was consult the list of topics she had created when storing his files. When he had finally agreed, and then thrown himself on the now uncluttered chair to sulk, he had seen her chalk one up for herself in the reflection of the window, and silently chortle with glee.

If he was honest, he reflected wryly, it really annoyed him the way she worked at shutting him out. It was the first time in his life that a beautiful woman had actually acted as if he did not exist. In spite of his better judgement, he had plotted and schemed, and was slowly forcing her to include him in her out-of-work activities. After all, they shared the same roof. It was only natural that they should socialize to some degree. And his schemes were working. He had actually maneuvered her into allowing him to watch the news on the television in *her* room.

It had taken some deviousness on his part, but that added to the challenge. First he had engaged her in conversation over events written up in *The Toronto Star* and *The Globe & Mail*. Then, one evening, when there was an item of sufficient interest to want to watch an update about it on the six o'clock news, he had rushed upstairs to watch while she had gone to her room. A few moments later, he had knocked on her door, and claimed that his television seemed to have gone on the fritz. He had asked if she would mind, just that once, if he could come in and watch. He had observed her expressive face as she considered his request. For a moment he thought that he had seen real apprehension on it, and had felt like a heel, but then dismissed the notion. After all, what harm could it do either of them if he spent a half hour with her watching the news.

Finally, she had let him in, and he had settled down in the armchair before the wall unit that contained the television. He had really been in luck that night because the station had finished the broadcast with a fifteen-minute special dealing with the economics of the Orient. They had watched it together, and then, without realizing it, she had entered into a lively discussion as they dissected the program.

The next night, he had prepared a tray of coffee and asked if he could watch the news again, and when she agreed, had taken it in. This time, there had been a sitcom immediately after the news that they had both enjoyed. Ever since, he had visited each evening for at least an hour, sometimes a little longer. To his annoyance, she was always the one to end the sessions, either by returning to the solarium to work, or by pointedly picking up a book to read. What was most unexpected about their evenings together was the fact that he really enjoyed her company.

He had learned quite a number of interesting things about her during these evenings. There was a semi-abstract painting of summer wildflowers standing in a crude container, somehow suggesting a child's gift of flowers. It hung above the entertainment center, expertly lit, so that when they sat and watched the television or chatted quietly, they could not help but look at it. She had asked if he knew anything about the artist, Martine Hébért. He did not, but because of her interest, he had lifted the picture down and turned it over. It was titled *Sarah's Bouquet* and dated some twelve years before. She had looked at it often, sometimes with a frown on her face. He had finally asked her what troubled her about the picture and her reply had been cautious. She thought that she might have seen it somewhere before.

With a sigh, Adam brought his attention back to his work. If he couldn't concentrate better than this, he thought, he would have to return to his study.

Lynn heard his sigh and glanced at the window. By angling her head just so, she could see her employer's reflection. Watching him dispassionately, she thought, he looks like an advertisement for Levi's in his red-plaid shirt and with his long, denim-clad legs stretched out before him. The evening lamplight caught the sun-polished red lights in his fair hair and lit the angles and planes of his face. Quite a handsome picture he made. However, she thought with a smirk, it would be the first Levi's ad in history that had a sexy model writing on a notepad instead of roaring off on a motor-bike or riding away on a stallion.

Annoyed that she was wasting time observing her employer, Lynn straightened her back and tried to settle down to work, but it was not easy. Every now and then, she could feel the hair on the back of her neck rise, and she knew that if she peeked at his reflection, she would see he was watching her. When she got tired of this inspection, she would deliberately turn around and smile at him, and he would have to return to work.

The man was too much. He made her nervous, always lurking about in the opposite corner of the room. It wasn't enough that he had started to work in the solarium; the man had managed to worm his way into her so-called *private* room. Now the evening coffee had suddenly become a ritual, and when she asked about *his* television, he had given her some song and dance about needing to get the Brownings' permission to purchase a new one. Last night, he had had the gall to suggest that they listen to one of the compact discs, and then, without waiting for her approval, had put it on, sat back down, closed his eyes and enjoyed himself.

What on earth was he about? Just for a moment, she wondered if he was attracted to her and was making some kind of move, but she dismissed the thought. She had found a copy of *Maclean's* with an article about Adam in Paris. It included a picture of him, and on his arm he had had a very glamorous French beauty. Adam would be attracted to sophisticated women, not a drudge of a typist with no memory, a wired jaw, and a cast on one foot. Why did she feel certain, then, that he was up to something?

*   *   *

Lynn stood before the bathroom mirror, an ice pack against her jaw. Was it only that morning that she had excitedly anticipated a fully mobile face with the removal of the wires? Well, tonight, she thought bitterly, it was a different story. The pain that was pounding along the right side of her jaw had driven her from bed, and was building in intensity. She looked at the container of pills that Dr. Dunlop had given her. One pill if the pain got bad, two if it was overwhelming. In the mirror, her newly completed face looked out at her and said, ''For heaven's sake, take one and ease your suffering.'' The part of her that did not know the face argued, ''Don't take the easy way. See how brave you really are. Deal with the pain.'' The new face lost the contest.

I'll go and do some more work, she thought. Maybe that will distract me from the pain. Moving quietly, she slipped into a housecoat, and taking her pills, went to the solarium. Instead of starting to work, she stood in the darkness and watched the outline of the trees tossing in the wind and listened to the rain pelt against the slanted windows. The pain increased, sweeping across her face in a fiery trail that made her gasp. In despair, she went to the kitchen and took out yet another cold pack. Returning to the solarium, she sat down on the chesterfield, held the cold pack to her jaw, and rocked back and forth. *Oh, God,* she thought, *Please help me. I can't stand this pain.* But tolerating the pain had become some kind of test. She would not give into it. In spite of herself, a moan of despair escaped her lips, and it was then Adam found her.

Waking with an idea, Adam had thrown on a track suit and tiptoed downstairs, careful not to make a noise in case he woke his assistant. In the kitchen he stopped with the notion of helping himself to one of her yogurt drinks when he heard a strange sound from the solarium.

His first thought was burglars, but surely, he reasoned, the security system would have gone off. He heard the sound again. That certainly was not a burglar. It sounded like someone in distress. What on earth could it be? he wondered. Moving on bare feet, he tiptoed to the door of the solarium and peeked in. It took his eyes a moment to adjust in the darkness, and then he saw her. She was sitting hunched over on the chesterfield, rocking back and forth, holding an ice pack to her face and moaning.

Going to her, he knelt, and murmured her name.

He startled her, and she sat bolt upright, horrified that he witnessed her humiliation. "Is it the pain?" he asked.

It was so obvious that she could not lie, but she thought as she nodded, *Oh, why did he have to hear me.*

He stood up and looked around. "Aren't the pills helping?" And then he noticed the container of pills. Tom had telephoned Adam and explained he had given Lynn six pills, and she was to be sure to take two every four hours if necessary but six pills were still in the container. Then what did she think she was doing? he thought angrily. "Why haven't you taken any of the pills?" he demanded.

She sprang up from the sofa and tried to get by him, but he caught her arm and pulled her around. "What are you trying to prove? Tom told you to take those pills."

She tried to pull away again and wept as she said, "I can't. How else am I going to tell what kind of person I am? I've got to find out whether I have courage or not."

"Whether you have courage or not?" he asked, and nearly shook her. "For heaven's sake, Lynn, Tom said that you showed great courage when dealing with your injuries and surgery. That is one reason he wanted me to employ you. He felt you deserved a chance to recuperate in reasonable surroundings."

Again she tried to pull herself free from his grip and mumbled, "You don't understand. There was no test of bravery in the hospital. They kept me drugged until the real pain had diminished. I need to know. I need to learn about myself."

Adam was losing all patience. "Tom told me that if you were having a bad time, I was to make sure that you took two of the capsules, and two of the capsules you will take, even if I have to shove them down your throat." He moved to the desk where the pill container sat, and removed two pills. There was a glass of water beside the container and he picked it up. Moving over to Lynn, he said, "Now, you have a choice. Either you take these capsules, or I phone Tom, and it is two o'clock in the morning."

She looked at him with those beautiful eyes. Even in the gloom of the sparsely lit solarium, they were eyes that you could lose yourself in. In the dim light, they were almost purple, the pupils dilated with anguish. But he had won. He had counted on the fact that she would not want to disturb his cousin. She bowed her head in submission, and held out her hand. He put the capsules on her palm and offered her the glass of water. Her body shuddered with a suppressed sob as she washed the capsules down, so that any sense of victory he might have felt was lost.

Sympathy at her distress swept over him, and without thinking he sat down and pulled her down beside him. "There is no need for you to suffer through this alone. Tom would not have wanted you to."

"You don't understand," she wept, "you just don't understand." Not knowing what else to do, he pulled her right up on his lap and rocked her as one would a child, stroking her hair, trying to calm her. As the paroxysms of sobs passed, she mumbled something. He thought he heard " 'Lone, so alone,'" and then he felt the drug take effect and her body relax against him. He continued to rock her, and the thought crossed his mind that it was many years since he had really been concerned about another's anguish. He held her closer, and her face snuggled into his shoulder. The fragrance of her hair and the warmth of her body reached out and surrounded him. Enough of this, he thought. Standing up with her in his arms, he took her into her room and placed her in the bed. She murmured for a moment, and turned her face into the softness of the pillow. He pulled up the duvet, leaned over and gently touched her cheek with the back of his hand.

Adam stood in the darkened living room for a long time. It was time, he thought, to consider seriously and honestly his reactions to this young woman. He had to admit that he felt an inordinate attraction to her, and yet she seemed so completely unaware of him. He also found himself quite fascinated by her beauty. It had been changing, emerging over the past few weeks, and he expected this change to continue. It wasn't just the perfection of her face, it was also the grace with which she moved and the air of fragility that she projected. And of course, there was the hint of mystery that tantalized him, the sense that all was not well. It stirred him to want to solve her mystery, and to rid her of that lost look she sometimes wore when she thought no one was looking.

Tonight, when she had expressed the need to test her courage, she had revealed more of herself. It was as if for some reason she did not know the limits of her personality. The mumbled *so alone* had suggested such desolation. All this had touched him deeply.

It was clear that his fascination with her was leading him into very deep water. He did not have time to become involved with someone, and certainly not someone who emanated innocence and vulnerability. He did not want a long-term relationship. He had never felt the need for one. His work, and the fact that he lived all over the world wherever his interests took him, had always made it easy to avoid serious relationships. What I need, he decided, is to get out socially, and find a willing companion. There certainly were lots of opportunities to meet people. There was the upcoming Board of Trade meeting at which he had finally agreed to speak. He'd get a date for that. He'd look up the reporter from *The Globe & Mail* that he had met in London last year. Furthermore, he would encourage Lynn to get out. The fact that they had been invited to Tom's for Thanksgiving dinner was a beginning.

Having settled the problem to his liking, Adam went upstairs to bed.

*   *   *

Lynn woke slowly, drifting in and out of a pleasant dream in which she was being held, rocked, treasured and cared for. She snuggled into her pillow, trying to sustain the feeling of happiness the dream evoked. But awareness of the bright light of day drew her away from it, and as she wakened, the scent of the one who had held her with such caring stayed near the surface of her consciousness. Finally, she woke, and was startled to see that it was after ten. It's odd, she thought, I haven't felt this drowsy since I've been here. Struggling to sit up, she yawned and a spasm of pain in the right side of her face cut off the movement. She touched the side of her face where Dr. Dunlop had had to do a little more than unwiring. It was no longer throbbing, but when she tried to open her jaw wide, it was still very sore.

Getting up, she went into the bathroom to inspect her face. The grip of the wires was really gone, and she could move her jaw up, down and sideways, although not as much as she would in time. Hurriedly, she stripped off her clothes, covered her cast with a plastic covering, and stepped into the shower. As the warm water poured down on her face, she moved it this way and that, and then she experimented with her voice. "How do you do? Hey, any one here?" The hot water on her face seemed to help the muscles relax, and the movement of her jaw became freer. Stepping out of the shower, Lynn continued to try out words and phrases as she toweled herself dry and dressed. By the time she left her room, she was on a high of enthusiasm and relief, for without a doubt, her voice and her face were going to be normal.

When she entered the kitchen, she found Adam at the counter making coffee. With great delight, she said clearly, "Good morning, Adam."

There was no doubt that he noticed the difference in her voice, for he turned toward her, one eyebrow raised, and said, "Well, you certainly sound happy today!"

"I am happy," she replied, "I'm free at last. Look." She made a few faces, and moved her jaw back and forth, up and down. "Listen. I can talk and sing." She tried a few lines of a popular song and did a little jig to the counter. "And today," she continued, "I am going to have a decent breakfast. Poached egg, toast with jam, and coffee in a proper cup. No straw."

She hummed a tune to herself as she proceeded to get a pan and cook her egg. Reaching past Adam who was still by the coffeemaker, she got the toaster and plugged it in. But even as she busied herself with the toaster, she noticed a scent. She stopped and concentrated for a minute. Adam, watching her expression, had to laugh. "Lynn, you remind me of a cat we had when I was a child. Whenever it tested the air, it used to stand quite still and wiggle its nostrils."

But even as he teased, she identified the scent. It was *his* aftershave. There was something else she could not place. And then it came to her in a flash. She had been dreaming of the scent when she woke up. But how could she be dreaming of Adam's aftershave? She had never noticed it before. She remembered something else. She had the vaguest recollection of Adam insisting she take her pills, and then holding her.

"Well?" he demanded, "what did you smell, my feline friend?"

Oh, Lord, she thought. I can't let him guess that it was him. And then, the good spirits of the morning took over, and mischief welled up in her. Looking him straight in the eye, with all the innocence she could muster, she said, "A skunk, I think."

Adam was taken aback. A skunk? A skunk in the kitchen? Then he noticed the glint in her eye, and to his amazement, what might be a dimple in her cheek. Was she teasing him? he wondered. Wait. It must be his aftershave she smelled. He had put on a little more than usual that morning. *A skunk?* Was she saying she smelled a *skunk*?

By this time, Lynn had placed her egg on top of her toast, and was heading to the table. With the sweetest of smiles, she asked, "Are you going to join me for coffee?" But he wasn't fooled for a minute. In spite of her look of innocence, that glint of mischief still lurked, and the dimple hovered on her cheek. Well, my little minx, he thought, two can tease. Picking up his coffee, he sat down at the table and said, "By the way, on Thanksgiving Sunday, we are expected at three o'clock."

She put down her cup and frowned at him. "What do you mean, *we* are expected at three o'clock? Where?"

"Why, Tom's, of course. They're having turkey and all the trimmings. Tom says Allison is quite excited. Since both their parents live elsewhere, Thanksgiving is usually quite a lonely time for them."

He watched the expressions flit across her face as she realized that she in no way would want to hurt

Tom's wife's feelings, and the words of refusal that he was sure she was formulating halted. Finally, she said, "It's very nice of them to include me in the invitation, but I really couldn't eat very well."

"You're managing quite well right now," he observe dryly. "You've just shoveled down that egg in record time." She darted him a dark look of displeasure. Darn him, she thought. He's enjoying this. He knows that I don't want to go. I'll try another tack. "I have nothing to wear."

"Well, if that is the case, I suggest that you take an afternoon this week and get something. There is nothing to stop you shopping now. Your speech seems normal and you walk easily with the cast. Take a taxi over to the mall."

Grinding her newly freed teeth together until she winced, she mumbled something about thinking about it, and started to clean up the kitchen table. And as she put away the last cup, an idea came to her. Let him have his moment, she promised herself. It would be short-lived.

Hurrying into the solarium, she settled down to work, and as usual, Adam wandered in and settled himself on the chair. He knew his presence annoyed her. She could see him watching her in the window's reflection. She worked quietly for a while. Then she began reciting "Mary had a little lamb. Its fleece was white as snow." She watched him frown as she repeated the entire rhyme three times.

She knew the moment he couldn't stand it any longer. I should have thought of this a long time ago, she thought, as he stood up and demanded, "What on earth are you doing?"

"Dr. Dunlop said that I was to exercise my voice and jaw quite a few times a day. Sorry if it bothers you." What could he say to that? Nothing, obviously, for he stomped out of the room.

She smiled so much that her face began to hurt, and standing up, raised her arms in a sign of victory. But as she sat down again, she noticed the sofa. She froze as the images came flooding back. It was not just that she had taken a pill. Now she could remember sitting on the chesterfield sobbing, and Adam taking her into his arms. No, not just into his arms, but onto his lap. She wasn't dreaming this morning. She was remembering how it felt to curl up against his chest and cuddle against his shoulder. That was why she remembered his aftershave. Darn pills, she thought, I am never taking one again. I don't care how bad the pain is. And then another question popped into her mind. How had she gotten to bed? Surely to goodness, he hadn't put her to bed?

She had to know. She marched over to the closed study door, knocked on it, walked in before her courage waned, and demanded, "Adam, did you put me to bed last night?"

He should have felt some victory at her obvious discomfort since she had had such fun driving him from the solarium, but the embarrassment on her face stopped him, and instead, he answered factually. "Yes, the painkillers knocked you out. Tom warned me that they might."

He watched her carefully as he spoke, but she covered any reaction carefully, and with a mumbled "Thank you," marched out.

*   *   *

A week later, Lynn had to admit that she had cut off her nose to spite her face. Adam had kept strictly away from the solarium, and much to her annoyance, she missed his presence. She realized now that it had taken her attention away from herself and her never-ending preoccupation with the problem of her lost memory. She had been so busy bristling at his various maneuvers that her mind had either been on him or her work.

To make matters worse, Adam seemed to have distanced himself from her even when they were not working. Oh, he was around as usual, ate with her about as much as he had before and assisted her with her work politely and efficiently, but something was different. She kept wondering if she had done something to earn his displeasure.

And here she was now, roaming around the house, lonely, because for the first time since she had come to work for Adam, he had gone out for the evening. She had been sitting watching the first of the Friday sitcoms when he stuck his head in the door to announce that he was going out, and not to be alarmed if he was very late.

She had not been able to contain her surprise when he stepped in the door, elegant in a dinner jacket. Without thinking, she had hopped up and with a grin on her face, had walked around him, examining him from every angle. She had let out a slow whistle—something she'd been practicing—and finished up with, "Wow! And what is the special occasion?"

For a few moments he let down his guard and grinned in response to her ribbing. "I'm going to the

Toronto Board of Trade annual dinner. Actually, I'm the guest speaker.''

''Well, I'm impressed,'' she said, and she had walked around him again, doing her sniffing act.

He'd laughed at that. ''You aren't, you know, you terrible girl. And I wonder what you smell *this* time.''

She had kept him waiting as long as she dared, and then, eyes twinkling with mischief, had answered, ''We--ll, I don't think it's a skunk, this time. Maybe . . . a lady killer?''

Really, he was fun to tease she had thought, as she watched him trying to figure out whether she was complimenting or insulting him. Then, with a shrug, he had smiled and bowed, ''If that means I look all right, then, thank you. However, I think it's probably more important that I am wise enough to give them some new and original thoughts on free trade.'' With that, he said good-bye and left.

And now she was wandering around the house, lonely for the first time. Finally, she returned to her room. She did not like being by herself. With Adam at home, working in the study or solarium, or even watching the news in her room, she felt anchored, safe, part of something. When he was there she had a sense of who she was: someone who could use a computer, a person interested in economics. With Adam gone, she could not avoid the emptiness, the loss of herself. How could she remember so much, how a computer worked, how to make coffee, the names of flowers, trees and birds, the objects about her, and yet remember nothing of herself, nothing but those hideous nightmares?

In despair, she turned to what she was sure she

knew. She picked up a large volume on economic theory, and focused her concentration on the subject.

It was later, as she was changing for bed and listening to the local television news, that her attention was caught by the words "world-famous Canadian economist, Frederick A. Stone." Turning to watch the screen, she saw that Adam was being interviewed in what seemed to be an after-dinner crowd in the lobby of the Harbour Castle Hotel. On his arm was the most gorgeous blond, and she stayed, attached to his arm, all the time that he was being interviewed. Like a leech, she thought viciously, and then was taken aback by her own reaction. Now why was she so annoyed about that? Adam certainly meant nothing special to her.

Life was not much better the next morning. She had been up for ages, had read *The Globe & Mail* from beginning to end, and was on her third cup of coffee when Adam entered the kitchen. Glancing up at him, she was surprised to see that he had not shaved and that he looked dreadful. She was just about to inquire about his health when he frowned and grumbled a barely civil greeting. It must have been some night, she thought. She decided that discretion was the better part of valor, and hastily tidied up the newspaper and left with the intention of slipping into the solarium. As she reached the door he called, "By the way, I'd like to see you after I've finished breakfast. It looks as if your job on my papers is nearly finished. We need to discuss where you are going to go next."

Lynn stopped in her tracks. *Her job was finished? Where was she going to go next?* Stunned, she looked back at him, but he had his nose buried in the newspaper. In a panic, she fled to the solarium. *Adam was dismissing her?* Frantically, she tried to come to terms with the idea. What on earth would she do? How would she get through any kind of job interview with no recollection of any other work experience than in this very room? She was not ready to go out into the world yet. She had no idea who her friends or her enemies were. As for any kind of mobility, she still had her cast on. Dr. Dunlop had intimated that her job was to last until the book was completed, but as far as she could see the book had not even been started. Adam was still firing ideas onto his piles of paper.

Five minutes passed, ten, and then fifteen, and still no Adam. The panic that had first swamped her gave way to indignation. Who did Adam Stone think he was, treating her this way? She had done his work accurately and quickly. How dare he dismiss her efforts so cavalierly. By the time she heard him get up from the chair in the kitchen and head toward the solarium, she had worked herself into a state of righteous indignation, and was ready to demand an explanation.

Adam came into the solarium with a sheet of paper in his hand. Without actually looking at her, he shoved the paper at her and growled, "Lynn, go to the study and see if you can find this information. Make a note of the material for me." With that, he turned and headed back toward the kitchen.

That did it. Not even a *please*. "Just who do you think you are, Adam Stone?" she stormed. "How dare you treat me this way!"

That stopped Adam in his tracks, but before he had even turned back, she raged on. "I've done your work just as you've asked. I've worked long hours so that it would be done quickly, and what do you do? You fire me! Without even a word of explanation.'' Even as Adam spun around, a look of confusion on his face, she shoved the paper at him and said grimly, ''Well, you can take your blasted paper and look up your own material.'' And with that, she stomped past him and rushed as quickly as she was able into her own room.

Adam stood, stunned, the wrinkled paper clutched in his hand. What was that all about? He grimaced. His head hurt. He didn't need an argument right now. All he needed was peace and quiet. And then, he thought again. What had she said? Fire her? Where on earth had she gotten a crazy idea like that?

With a sigh of resignation, Adam headed for her room. The door was closed, so he knocked and called, ''Lynn, what in the name of heaven are you talking about?'' When there was no answer, he shrugged his shoulders and thought, I seem to be in trouble already, I might as well go in. He knocked again, and threw the door open.

Lynn was standing before a window, her arms wrapped tightly around her waist. His head still aching, confused and in a belligerent mood, Adam marched over to her and demanded, ''I asked you what on earth are you talking about?''

When she turned to speak to him, he was appalled. Her face was ashen. She whispered, ''I want to know why you are dissatisfied with my work. I know that I was out of line doing my voice exercises in your solarium, but I was only teasing. I can't think of any other reason why you would want to fire me. I thought you hired me to work on your manuscript.''

Adam groaned. Why, today, when jackhammers

were bouncing off his skull, and he was still recovering from making a monumental ass of himself with the bright young reporter, did he have to have a row with Lynn? After all, it was Lynn's fault he had made such a fool of himself. In spite of every message his mind and body had sent him, he had doggedly pursued the notion that a new female in his life would counter the endless fascination he was developing for the very angry young woman before him. When it had come to the crunch, he had found himself bored and disinterested, and facing a very annoyed date. No amount of fast talking had kept him from leaving her apartment with the proverbial egg all over his face.

Counting to ten, and taking a long breath, he sighed and said, "Lynn, there must be a misunderstanding. I don't know where you got the idea I wanted to fire you. The thought never crossed my mind. In fact, I wanted to discuss a promotion."

"But you said that my job on your papers was nearly finished, and that you wanted to discuss *where* I was to go next." To his utter dismay, he could hear the fear in her voice, and see that she visibly trembled. Taking her hands in his, he led her to the chaise longue she used, and then sat down beside her in his chair. Still holding her hands, he said, "Lynn, I have the most dreadful hangover, and I guess the words came out the wrong way. All I wanted to do was to discuss how we would handle the next stage of the work. The last thing I need or want is for you to stop working for me. You have saved me hours of time already."

Color returned to her face as she realized what he was saying. "I'm sorry. I guess I panicked. It's just that I enjoy what I do, and I was looking forward to working on the book. I was so disappointed.'' *And terrified,* she thought to herself.

He still held her hands, and his grip steadied her. ''I planned to promote you to research assistant. The paper I gave you was the first piece of research I wanted you to try to do. I'm pretty sure that I can train you to do a good job.'' She sat, those lovely violet eyes looking at him warily. ''Don't you want the job?''

And still she sat, watching him, weighing her decision, obviously considering matters that he could not imagine, and then she smiled that devastating smile that made his heart turn over, and whispered, ''Yes, Adam. Oh, yes.'' And she thought to herself, you will never know how much I want this job. Safety, security, and the thought of working with someone as exciting as you—all in one.

Adam, as he breathed a sigh of relief, felt sure that there was more to this than just a misunderstanding. What could have caused that overreaction?

With the release of the tension between them, his headache magically disappeared and he suddenly felt the need for action. Standing up, he took her hand and pulled her to her feet. With a grin, he announced, ''Come on. You and I are going to celebrate your new status. Let's go over to the mall and have brunch. After, if you like, we can do some shopping, or just wander around and watch the world go by.''

The mall, she thought in a panic. *On a Saturday noon!* In spite of her successful trip after her bandages had been removed, she still felt uneasy about leaving the house. She had a fear that someone might be looking for her.

He was watching her expectantly, sure of her response. How could she do otherwise than agree after making such a fuss over what seemed to have been a perfectly innocent statement? Maybe I have stayed inside too long, she thought. Maybe I'm becoming paranoid.

Well, she decided with a sudden surge of courage, I have to reenter the real world sooner or later. It might as well be today. With a nod she agreed, and muttered something about freshening up. "Put on your fuchsia track suit," he suggested, and when she looked surprised, he grinned and said, "It's my favorite."

That really surprised her. He actually noticed what she wore. Amazing! Before the conversation could become more confusing, he walked to the door and said, "Fifteen minutes. I'll telephone and see if I can get a reservation at Tony's."

In the end, the experience was not all that bad. The mall was busy but so full of ordinary people—families with children, teenagers, elderly people—that it was difficult to imagine that anyone could be watching her with the intent to harm. Everyone was too occupied with their own shopping needs, too busy getting ready for Thanksgiving. Lynn relaxed and began to enjoy herself.

The meal they had together was a pleasant change from the usual work-as-you-eat lunch they had been in the habit of having. Adam set out to entertain her with tales of his travels in Europe and the Orient, and in no time she had forgotten all about her fears. Over coffee, he outlined the various topics on which he wanted her to gather data. For the present, it seemed most of it could be gained through the modem, fax machine and telephone. She refused to think about the need to go out of the house. When that time comes, she thought, I will deal with it.

When their coffee was finished, Adam presented her with an envelope. Opening it, she found an amazing amount of money and a typed salary statement with the appropriate deductions. Her eyes opened wide. "Adam? What is this?"

"Let's face it," he said, "for some time now you have been doing more than just entering facts into the computer. You have employed skills far beyond those that I hired you to use. This is just back pay for working for me as an assistant." When she looked as if she was going to argue, he continued, "From now on, I will not only expect you to research material, I will want you to handle all incoming calls, to keep my diary and organize any engagements as well as keeping up with the manuscript. I think that you will find that you will earn every cent."

And with those words he stood, assisted her from her chair, and guided her from the restaurant. With Adam helping her, they were able to spend the afternoon slowly walking around the mall, and Lynn found that she actually enjoyed herself. She purchased a new outfit, and they stopped in a shoe store where Adam waited patiently while she bought a pair of low-heeled pumps and nylons for the next day. By the time they reached home, there was a sense of harmony between them that neither had felt before.

That evening Lynn headed for the solarium, anxious to look up the notorious assignment that Adam had given her, and determined to finish the last of the paper piles. Adam, for his part, disappeared into the study, eager to begin to write. He barely acknowledged her when she looked up the material, only muttered something about being on a roll. He was still hard at it when Lynn disposed of the last pile of paper, tidied up the desk, and headed for bed.

It's been a red-letter day, she thought. Not only have I been given a promotion, I moved around the mall with hardly a thought of danger. Let's hope I can do as well at the Dunlops, but the very thought of the coming day caused her stomach to clench in apprehension.

Lynn slept in the next morning, and after a leisurely breakfast with Adam, wandered back into the solarium. Adam followed, and when she sat down at her desk and reached out to turn on the computer, he stilled her hand. When she looked up in surprise, he announced, "No work today. It's Thanksgiving Sunday. Go and get your jacket on, and we'll go for a short walk. By then, it will be time to get ready to go over to Tom's."

She was about to object, but a glance out the solarium window convinced her that he was right. Over the past few days, the woods at the back of the property had flamed into color. If the trees in the streets were anything like them, it would be a delightful walk. It would be her first sally out along the streets since her accident, but with Adam there for protection, she would be safe, so she shrugged off her worries and joined him.

The air was crisp, the sky cobalt blue, and everywhere trees and shrubs were ablaze with color. Varieties of maples ran the spectrum from yellow to orange to the deepest crimson. The duller red of oaks was made vibrant by the sun. The yellow of birches and the deep green of cedars and pines completed the picture. It was not just the trees that celebrated the passing of summer. Many of the exotic gardens along the street had rare shrubs that added their russets, tans and purples to the scene.

They walked for quite a while, not talking, just enjoying the autumn display, breathing in the keen, fresh air and listening to the crisp rustle of leaves at their feet. Finally, Adam stopped before a stand of maples that glowed like rubies in the sun, and said softly, "This is what I missed in Europe. The vivid autumn sky and those incandescent colors. Thank goodness we celebrate Thanksgiving Day in October when our season is at its best." Turning, he smiled down at her and said, "Let's go down this street. There is a ravine at the end we can investigate."

Until that moment, Lynn had not really looked at the street, but when she did, a chill ran down her spine, and she could feel the hair on her neck stand up with apprehension. She was stunned by her reaction and Adam noticed it. When he asked what was wrong, she couldn't explain, and covered up by claiming that her leg had suddenly started to ache. Full of contrition that he had forgotten about her leg, he led them toward home. But all the way back, she wondered what it had been about the street that seemed to scream danger.

When they returned, Lynn had time for a rest, then dressed carefully for dinner at the Dunlops. She had to admit that she enjoyed a chance to dress up. It was a whole new experience to put on the stocking that she pulled up comfortably on her good leg. The delphinium-blue blouse and skirt she had purchased fitted her perfectly, and she reveled in the texture of the silk shirt on her skin, and the way the lined skirt fell about her waist and hips as if made especially for her.

She had also bought some makeup and gingerly applied it. A dusky eyeshadow and slight blusher added some color to her face. Mascara added length to her eyelashes so that her eyes glowed like jewels. Startled by the effect of the makeup, she almost washed it off, and then realized that it was time to go. Squaring her shoulders, she walked to her door when she heard Adam knock.

Her stomach was a-flutter with butterflies, and she could feel herself blushing as she opened the door. She was disarmed by Adam when he whistled, and then walked around her imitating her as he sniffed the air. "And who do we have here? Certainly not my typist. It must be my new research assistant who has just spent every cent she has. Wow! Nice leg, too. I think that we are going to have quite a surprise for Tom."

She smiled at this nonsense and regained her composure. "I'm afraid I'm about to spoil the effect by having to wear my ski jacket. Your research assistant didn't have time or the money to buy a coat."

In spite of this, she had to admit that she felt quite grand when Adam helped her into her jacket and offered her his arm as they left the house for the waiting taxicab. As they traveled down the Don Valley Parkway, Lynn got up the nerve to ask why Adam did not have a car of his own. He turned and with a grin that quite charmed her, said, "Sheer laziness. I just haven't felt the need. You know how busy I've been. Anyway, taxis are easier."

The Dunlops lived in an older area of Toronto called The Beaches, popular because of the houses that were individual and varied, and its nearness to the Lake Ontario shore where its residents enjoyed the boardwalk that edged its beach.

Their home was a large blue clapboard affair with Victorian towers and gingerbread trim. A massive maple and oak spread vibrant branches over the leaf-strewn lawn, and Lynn could not help but think that it must be a wonderful place in which to raise children.

Any shyness Lynn felt as they made their way up to the Dunlops' door was soon forgotten when Adam's cousin appeared and greeted her. He took her jacket and then walked around her just as Adam had, raising his eyebrows and whistling. With a grin, he said to Adam, "Can this be the same black-and-blue creature I sent to you? How do you manage to get any work done with a typist as beautiful as this?"

Before Lynn could react to the teasing, Adam had corrected his cousin. "Not typist, Tom, but research assistant!"

As they made their way into a spacious living room, Adam continued, "You not only found me a beautiful typist, you found me a very clever assistant who I believe can save me a lot of time confirming facts I need, and who can also catch every error in logic I make. At the rate we are going, we should have the book finished in no time. I am in your debt, dear cousin."

It pleased her to hear Adam say that she was good at her job, and she wondered, does he really think I am beautiful? After all, he must have met many beautiful women in his day. Certainly the one on the television was gorgeous. But, she thought gloomily, is the fact that I have a pretty face really important when I have no idea about the real substance and character behind this face?

Her thoughts were interrupted by the entrance of Tom's wife, Allison, and their two children. Allison was a vivacious redhead whose pixie-like features were covered with a multitude of freckles. She welcomed them into the room, insisted that Lynn sit on the chair with the footstool, and then introduced the two children. Their oldest child, Anne, a feminine version of Tom, was eight years old and very serious, while their youngest child, Nick, had his mother's coloring but his father's infectious sense of mischief. A dog of mixed ancestry completed the family circle, and much to Lynn's surprise settled by her chair where it could have its head scratched.

From the minute they sat down in the living room Lynn felt at home. As predinner drinks were served to everyone but Lynn, who had to sip Perrier because of her head injury, their shy, dark-haired daughter passed appetizers while the two cousins entertained them with tales of their own childhoods. As each cousin vied with the other in describing their outrageous adventures, Lynn could not help but note the similarities and differences between the two men. Both were tall and lean and had similar profiles, but where Adam was fair with gray eyes, Tom was dark and had blue eyes. Lynn learned Adam's father was a diplomat, often posted to distant places, and that Adam had frequently stayed with Tom's family rather than be taken to the far corners of the world. The experience did not seem to have hurt him, she thought, because she picked up the sense that not only had he enjoyed his time with his cousin, he had been loved by his cousin's parents as well as his own. Maybe that is what has given him such confidence in himself, she thought. I wonder if I have a family, parents, and cousins with whom I have shared good times. Somehow, I don't think so. If they existed, they would surely have hunted for me. With some annoyance, she tried to shake off her introspection.

The meal was everything that a Thanksgiving dinner should be. There was turkey and cranberries, vegetables and gravy, and the inevitable pumpkin pie. As the meal was eaten, the conversation continued with everyone joining in, even Lynn. When the last bit of pie had been cleaned off her plate, Lynn smiled ruefully at Allison and said, "I couldn't eat another thing if I tried. That was a wonderful meal. I don't remember ever having a better one." She had used the last phrase automatically, without thought, and was stunned when Allison's face lit up with excitement as she said, "Oh, you've got your memory back!"

The words hung in the air and to Lynn's horror, Adam heard them and turned toward Lynn. "You lost your memory?" When she found herself unable to form a reply to his question, Adam turned to Allison and demanded, "What do you mean, has she got her memory back?"

It was clear from Allison's guilty face that there was something here worth pursuing, and Adam, Lynn knew, would not stop now until he had the whole truth. Helplessly, she looked at Tom for assistance. Clearing his throat, Tom rose from the table and said, "I think it's time that we had a conference. Let's go into the living room, and over coffee, with Lynn's permission, I'll explain.'' Lynn stood, grabbed some dishes and headed for the kitchen. She was followed by a very embarrassed Allison. ''Lynn, can you ever forgive me? I thought from what you said that your memory must have returned. Also, I didn't realize that Adam knew nothing about it.''

''Actually, it will be a relief to have Adam know,'' she assured her. ''It has been very hard covering up my ignorance. Adam's astute, and he has sensed that there is something different about me. He just hadn't worked it out.'' And with that, she insisted on continuing to help her hostess tidy up the kitchen and load the dishwasher. Anything to keep from telling her tale to Adam. All too soon, the coffee was ready and taken into the living room by Allison. Feeling like a condemned woman ready to face the firing squad, Lynn settled on the chair kept for her, and waited.

By unspoken agreement, Tom took over the role of chairperson of this supposed conference. ''I think that it would be best if we started at the beginning. That's if you agree, Lynn, that we should explain about your memory to Adam.''

He waited for her reply, and she thought to herself, I don't have to explain, but then again, Adam committed an act of faith when he offered me a job as a research assistant. The least I can do is return that trust. If he decides when he hears the entire story that I am unfit to assist him, then I will have to accept his decision.

''I think we should explain,'' she said to Tom. ''I would not like Adam to think that we were trying to dupe him in some way.'' She saw Adam frown at this but went on, ''Would you begin as you suggested.''

Before starting he refilled his coffee, and then, as if to assure Allison that she had not made a very serious error, pulled her toward him on the sofa, and with his arm around her, began.

"On August seventeenth of this year, at eleven o'clock at night, an emergency call came into Sunnybrook Hospital just as I was leaving from checking a tricky piece of reconstruction I had done that day. We were told that a massive pileup had occurred on Highway 401 just east of Toronto, and that several people with very serious injuries were due to arrive by ambulance almost immediately. The ambulance crew was specific in stating that there was one person with head wounds who had sustained serious injury to her jaw, and so I was requested to be ready for surgery."

"When I first saw Lynn, she had multiple injuries to her head, ribs and leg. The leg and ribs were straightforward, and were dealt with easily. Her face and head were quite another problem. After X rays and a CAT scan, it was ascertained that although there had been much damage to the bones in her jaw and nose, and some nasty cuts to her scalp, there appeared to be no damage to the brain or spine. I was then faced with the problem of trying to reconstruct her jaw. It was decided to leave the nose area until later."

Lynn glanced at Adam. As she suspected, he was concentrating completely on the story Tom was telling. Looking at the doctor, she was surprised to see that he looked somewhat embarrassed and seemed not quite sure how to proceed. "The next part of my tale is a little unusual. I had planned to explain it to Lynn when she came in for her final checkup this week, however, I think I will have to confess now.''

Confess what? Lynn wondered. Good grief! Wasn't there enough mystery about her case without more to confess? She looked at the doctor in alarm as he continued. "When we examined your jaw, Lynn, it was evident that you had a rare congenital condition in which the jaw drops and grows back during adolescence. It is a condition that is curable now, although the surgery is unpleasant. It was surprising to us that it had not already been done on a young woman of your age as it is considered necessary surgery and recently had been covered under the provincial health service. Anyway, I decided, with the total agreement of the plastic surgeon who had looked in, that while I was repairing the two breaks to your jaw on the right side of your face, that I would also realign both sides of your jaw. It seemed criminal not to. Consequently, Lynn, one of the reasons why you might not have recognized yourself is that your face looks quite different around the jaw. You could not tell any difference from that very poor picture on your driver's license, but if and when your memory returns, you will get quite a surprise. Had I realized that we were dealing with a case of amnesia, I think that I would have refrained from doing the realignment. I am hoping that the change in your face did not contribute to your memory loss.''

Lynn listened to this confession with surprise. So she had not looked as she looked now. If her jaw was different, she wondered if her nose was different, too. But after all, she had chosen her nose, and she had felt no hesitation in making her selection.

Noting the look of concern on the doctor's face, she reassured him, "Honestly, Dr. Dunlop," and when he frowned, she corrected herself, "Tom, you could do anything to my face. I have complete confidence in you. If it hadn't been for you, I would still be in the coma."

At this statement, all eyes focused on her, so she explained. "My first conscious memory is Tom's voice complaining that I wouldn't look at him and that I had wiggled my ears. That particular piece of nonsense made me open my eyes and thus the coma ended."

Tom looked relieved, and continued. "You must realize, Adam, no one knew that Lynn had lost her memory. First she was in a coma, then heavily medicated, and finally very restricted by her wired jaw. By the time her face had healed sufficiently for her to speak, she had decided to tell no one about her amnesia. It was only a lucky guess on my part that I knew about it. And after listening to her reasons, I felt I had to respect her wishes not to tell anyone."

Adam interrupted Tom's story and turned to Lynn, "I don't understand. Was there no one that came to claim you after the accident?"

Trust Adam, Lynn thought, to go to the heart of the story. Tom answered for her. "We found out that Lynn was a secretary for a civil servant in Ottawa. Or I should say, the police found out. According to them, Lynn was a very private person who had not made friends with the other people in the office. She lived alone, and, it seems, without any reason except that she wanted to see Toronto, left a good job in Ottawa to come to Toronto. The only other information the police supplied was that Lynn came from Glace Bay, Nova Scotia, and that she had been raised by a grand-mother who was now dead. She had also worked in Quebec. We know, too, that she was a baseball fan because she had a ticket to the Blue Jays' game for the day after the accident and a reservation at the SkyDome hotel for two nights. That was all we had to go on.''

At that point, the two children came into to say good-night and get ready for bed. Lynn breathed a sigh of relief. They could stop this tale right now without telling any more and Adam would be satisfied.

But Adam was not satisfied. All through Tom's re-counting of her accident, he had been aware that Lynn was uptight. She sat straight and tense in the big arm-chair. And when the children came in, her relief was obvious. Her story intrigued him—amnesia! All the trappings of fiction. He had always doubted that such cases really occurred. Yet there was no doubt in his mind that his cousin and Lynn were both sincere. She really did not remember anything about her past. As soon as the children had departed for bed, he turned to Tom and said, ''Were there no more clues? It seems strange that she can recall all her skills and yet not recall her life in Ottawa.''

Lynn heard the question with a sinking heart. In all innocence, Tom continued, as interested in her case as Adam was, and he certainly had every right to, she thought bitterly to herself, because she had set no lim-its on the evening's discussion.

''There were certain very unusual features of Lynn's case that caused concern to the staff. At first, it seemed that we had all the information that we needed, but then, the nightmares began.''

''Nightmares?'' asked Adam.

Tom gave Lynn a reassuring smile and replied, ''Nightmares. Great, wild, blood-chilling nightmares. When Lynn came out of the coma, she entertained her roommate nightly with them. It was hard to get another patient to share her room. That is how I caught on to the fact that she had amnesia. I still find it hard to believe no other medical staff figured it out. She was very astute about how she handled us.''

Lynn sat there willing Tom to end his tale, but of course Adam wasn't going to leave it there, and turning to Lynn, he asked, ''What did you dream about?''

Unable to look at him while she answered the question, she occupied herself by scratching the dog who had returned to the side of her chair. ''I . . . uhmmm . . . dream that I am tied up in a dark, confined place. I can't get free, although I try very hard. I dream it over and over.'' With a sigh, she looked up at him. ''I have no idea what all this means, but it seems very real in the dream.''

She could see Adam's mind literally ticking with this information. With a feeling of dread, she knew that he would chew it over, trying to make sense of it. She knew how his mind worked when he had a problem. Giving her a very direct look, Adam asked, ''Do you think that you are recalling an incident that really happened?''

She found that she couldn't lie to him. ''I'm afraid I know that the incident must have happened.''

''You mean that you do remember something before the accident?'' he asked sharply.

At this point, Tom intervened. "What Lynn means is that there were very deep abrasions on her wrists and ankles when she arrived at the hospital. They had obviously not been caused by the accident, although they were recorded as being quite recently inflicted. Since they were not life-threatening, and Lynn's injuries demanded immediate attention, they were completely ignored. It was after the nightmares began that they became significant."

Adam looked over at Lynn, and she could not help but pull down the sleeve of her blouse. To her dismay, he caught the surreptitious action, got up and came over to her chair. Bending over, he picked up her wrist and pulled back her sleeve. The scars had faded somewhat, but they were still there, silent witness to her story. She tried to pull her hand away from Adam's grip, but he held on and absentmindedly stroked the red lines with the pad of his thumb. "Did you tell the police about this? Obviously, someone was out to harm you."

Lynn found herself mesmerized by the motion of his thumb on the inside of her wrist, so much so that it took her a minute to focus on his question. When she realized its intent, she responded with alarm.

"Adam, I did not want to go to the police then and I do not want to now. I want to leave this entire question of my memory until I am completely recovered from the accident and your book is finished. Then I will deal with the scars and the nightmares. Until then, I want to try and forget the whole mystery. I have enough on my plate right now. I want to recall or learn, whatever the case may be, as much as I can about economics. That is one thing that I feel I did know at one time. Your subject material seemed familiar from the very beginning, and working with you has made it easy to relearn it. When I feel confident about that, then I'll turn to the mystery.''

And with that, Adam had to be satisfied. But Lynn knew that he was not ready to let it go. All the way home in the car, she could tell that he was mulling it over. The entire conversation had upset her, and as they drove home through a very windy night with scurrying clouds covering and uncovering a bright, full moon, she felt uneasy. When she got out of the car, the flickering light of the moon and the dark shadows made by wind-tossed trees filled her with inexplicable apprehension. It was with relief that she entered the house and moved to the safety of her room.

Adam cleaned up his study desk and stood up. Looking at his watch, he was not surprised to see that it was two in the morning. What an effort it had been to concentrate tonight after the fascinating story of Lynn's loss of memory and unexplained injuries. Over and over the strange tale of scarred wrists and nightmares had interfered with his work. Just looking at those scars on her wrists had filled him with anger. The thought that someone could treat her that way caused an unexpected surge of rage.

With a sigh, he ran his hand through his hair. There was nothing he could do right now, and from the look on Lynn's face on the way home, possibly there would never be anything he could do, for she made it obvious that she was unhappy that he knew about it.

He walked into the darkened solarium and stopped for a minute to watch the scene outside. Clouds were racing across a bright moon that silvered the wind-tossed trees at the back of the yard. The leaves will be blown off, he thought with regret, and that will be the end of the color for another year. Even as the thought crossed his mind, he was aware of the swish of leaves against the sloped glass of the solarium. With a shrug, he turned and headed down the hall toward the stairs.

An unusual sound brought him to a stop just as he reached the stairs. What was it? he wondered. Not the wind. Something banging. He stood still and listened. The sound seemed to be coming from the living room. But what was in there to make such a sound? Quietly, he went into the living room. In the faint light from the window, he could see that nothing was disturbed. Then he realized the sound seemed to be coming from Lynn's room. Alarmed now, he started across the living room when he heard it—a high keening sound that made the hair on the back of his neck stand up. Before he could reach the door, there was a crash.

Adam sprang to the door, threw it open and turned on the light that illuminated the sitting area. From beyond, the keening rose again, and he was appalled to see Lynn thrashing about on the bed. The coverlet had slipped onto the floor and her bedside lamp lay beside the bed. A nightmare, he thought. She's having a nightmare!

Calling her name he raced to the bed, but Lynn was completely unaware of him. She was gasping and he could see that she was wet with perspiration. As he moved to touch her, she tightened her body and wailed that same eerie cry.

Clasping her by the arms, he called her name, but

he knew from the glazed look in her eyes that she did not see him. At the touch of his hand, her terror became more pronounced and she fought him with all her strength. He shook her as he called her name, then tried pulling her upright in the hope that he would break the hold of the dream.

He knew the minute that reality began to take over. Her eyes focused, and she seemed to recognize him for the first time. And then, with a great heaving breath she cried, "Adam," and threw herself against him. All he could do was hold her clasped tightly against him, stroke the tousled head that was hidden against his shoulder, and rub her shuddering back until her breathing became more normal. At the same time, he was aware of the slightness of her, the terrified pounding of her heart and the faint fragrance of wildflowers that he associated with her.

Finally, she brought her arms up between them and leaned back to look at him. The terror of the dream still lurked in her eyes, and her face was wet with tears. He could not help himself. Anything, he thought, to distract her from her fear. Gently, he brushed the tears from her face with his fingers, and bent down and kissed her. A kiss of tenderness, meant to heal and assure. But as he stroked and tasted and caressed it became much more, and he wanted to fold her silken-clad body to him. A sound from her brought him back to his senses. What in heaven's name was he doing, he wondered, as he gazed down at her face. In those violet eyes all sign of terror had been replaced by one of complete bewilderment. Oh help, he thought, had she never been kissed before?

Then he acted. Reaching down, he lifted the crumpled duvet from the floor, and in one motion, wrapped it around her and picked her up. With quick, decisive strides, he carried her into the kitchen, turned on the light and set her on one of the stools. When he was sure that she was settled securely, he turned toward the counter and announced, "I'm going to make some warm cocoa for both of us. I think we need it."

Risking a glance at her, he was startled to see the bemused look still on her face and her fingers touching her lips. What to do now? he wondered. Taking a big breath, he turned to her and said, "Sorry. It was just a kiss. I wanted to distract you. I hope you didn't mind."

Just a kiss, she thought. He could dismiss what he did in that room as just a kiss? She had felt its power right to the tips of her toes. She hadn't known that her lips could contain such sensation. Just a kiss! And it wasn't just the kiss. The memory of his scent, the roughness of his shirt, the beat of his heart and the outline of his body against her were all part of that kiss. She glanced at him from under lowered lashes. Hadn't he felt anything? He certainly looked as if nothing had happened, standing there stirring the milk.

Turning toward her, he asked, "What was the dream about, Lynn?"

The sensation of panic returned and she shut her eyes in the hope that the images would fade, but they did not. She could see the nightmare vividly. She was running in and out of trees, stumbling over shrubs and rocks, dodging into shadows, trying to escape from someone. But the night was moonlit, and clouds were racing across the sky, giving her precious moments of safety and terrifying moments of exposure. She could hear someone crashing behind her, cursing her as he pursued. But who? she thought desperately. Who was chasing her?

"Lynn? Do you know?"

There was no use hiding it from him, she thought. No use at all. "Someone was chasing me through the night in what seemed to be some kind of wild place. There were trees, rocks and shrubs, and I was stumbling and falling. The moon kept coming out from behind the clouds, and I was afraid that he would catch me."

"Who would catch you, Lynn?"

"I don't know." The answer seemed so weak. Surely if she could remember a dream with such detail, she could identify the enemy. Unable to look at him, she took her milk and sipped it, lost in the misery of her predicament.

Then he surprised her. "Lynn, would you like me to leave the book so that we can concentrate on discovering the answers to your questions?"

Startled, she looked at him. "Why would you want to do that? You know that you have publisher's deadlines."

For a moment he continued to stir the milk, then finally turned toward her. He gave her a long, level look from those gray eyes of his, as if weighing his response. "I don't think that I could bear to see you have another such nightmare. I doubt that you could survive it. Quite frankly, I think that you would die of fright."

She was stunned by his answer. He would do that for her? But, of course, she couldn't let him. His book was important. It needed to be written. But she was touched deeply. Looking him square in the eye, she lied. "The dreams I had earlier were even worse, but I survived. I want to see your book finished. By then, I may have remembered everything. And I'm safe here. But thank you anyway."

Lynn woke slowly the next morning, aware of a great sense of fatigue and a general soreness everywhere. With a groan, she turned over and tried to slip back to sleep, too weary to think of getting up. For a few minutes she dozed, but the brightness of the room told her that it was late, and with a sigh she sat up. I feel as if I've been hit by a train, she thought. I wonder if I'm getting the flu? And then she remembered. The nightmare! Frightening images drifted vividly through her consciousness. With a shudder, she got out of bed, and grabbing some clothes, headed for the bathroom. Too tired to go through the rigmarole of showering with her cast on, she settled with a quick wash and dressed. Then she headed for the kitchen.

She poured herself a coffee that Adam had thoughtfully left prepared in the coffeemaker, and helped herself to some granola. Even that seemed an effort, and she pushed the cereal around her plate with disinterest. She wondered what Adam thought today. Maybe he was reconsidering whether or not she was a risk. From all the evidence, she could have been involved in something criminal; the drug trade, for instance. After all, your average citizen doesn't carry around memories of violence.

You are depressed, she thought. *Shake yourself out of it. You're just tired.* Then Adam wandered in.

Grumpily, she watched him as he poured out a coffee. It annoyed her that she could not seem to take her eyes off him. Today he wore a black turtleneck sweater and tight-fitting blue jeans. She found herself fascinated by the play of muscles that rippled along his arms and shoulders. He turned and studied her pale face and dejected stance. "Do I take it that you are suffering the effects of last night?"

She tried a weary smile, but he wasn't fooled. With a grin, he added, "I thought that I had found a cure for your nightmare."

The kiss. She'd forgotten the kiss. How could she have? She could feel a blush sweeping over her face as she busied herself with what was left of her granola. She refused to look at him. It was all right for him to tease. The kiss had obviously been an everyday event for him.

He picked up his cup of coffee, came closer and sat down, and said gently, "How are you feeling today?"

Looking at him, she shrugged ruefully. "I feel sore all over. It will pass, I'm sure, as soon as I get to work."

"Look," he said. "I want you take it easy today. Only work if you really feel like it. And one more thing." Oh-oh, she thought, here it comes. Adam is having second thoughts. But he surprised her yet again. "I have arranged a contract with a local taxi company. You are to use this company, and only it. All you need to do is telephone them, give them the contract number and they will give you priority. I don't want you walking these streets on your own once that cast is off, and I do not want you using strange taxi services."

Her eyes flew to his face. He looked quite grim as he continued. "I want to be sure that you are safe. I would get a car and drive you myself, but that would mean that you could only travel when I was free. Over the next few weeks you will have to go to various agencies and pick up information for me that I can't get from my database. I want to know that you are in good hands while you are out."

She couldn't let him go to that expense. Taxis were an extremely expensive way to travel. He watched as a mulish expression crossed her face. "Adam, you are making my problem yours, and there is no reason for it. I can manage, thank you." And with that, she stood up, picked up her dishes and headed for the sink.

She never made it past him. He caught her arm, almost making her drop the dishes in her hand. Giving her one of his most ferocious scowls, he said in the silkiest of tones, "If you want to work for me, you will do as I say. No taxi, no job!"

Well, he had her there, she thought. With as much dignity as she could muster, she shook her wrist free of his grip and with her nose in the air, headed for the kitchen sink. "If you insist," she mumbled, as she deposited the dishes and fled into the solarium. Settling down at her desk, she became aware that the feeling of fatigue had passed. There was nothing like a battle of wills with Adam to liven one up.

Lynn eased back in her chair and twisted her neck to relieve the tension. It was midnight, and she had been working for three hours without a break, but it had been worth every second. In the five weeks since Thanksgiving they had performed wonders, working together harmoniously and efficiently, and tonight she had completed the final draft of the second chapter of Adam's book.

Setting up the printer, she got up and went into the kitchen to make some decaffeinated coffee. What a day, she thought, as she measured out the required amount and set the machine in motion. It seemed that she had been busy from the moment that she had awakened.

That morning she had taken another step toward building confidence in herself. For some time, she had been aware that she had little dress sense. On several occasions she had gone shopping with every intention of coming home with a new wardrobe, and yet, when she made a selection and tried on the clothes, she was always disappointed. It was as if she had had very little experience purchasing anything but jeans and sweaters. Finally, in desperation, she had telephoned Allison and begged her to join her for lunch, and then to give her some advice in selecting clothes. To her relief, Allison had agreed, and they had met in a restaurant she suggested. When she explained her problem to Allison, and also the fact that the amount she had to spend was limited, Allison had suggested several secondhand stores that dealt in high-quality clothes.

Traveling by taxi, they had visited the shops and picked up several skirts, slacks and blouses, even a bathing suit. They had also picked up a very stylish dress that would grace any cocktail party or dressy dinner. Allison had taught Lynn to see for herself that blues, purples, strong blue-greens, pure yellows and vibrant reds suited her best. Just as they were leaving the second store, Allison had spied a stylish pair of wool tartan walking shorts suitable for casual winter wear. In seconds, she had convinced Lynn that these were just the thing to wear when she was working. Lynn had agreed, they would be a happy change from her three track suits and the shirts and jeans she had purchased by herself.

Lynn poured the coffee into a thermos and placed it along with a mug and a plate of biscuits on a tray and headed back into the solarium. Placing the tray on the table beside the sofa, she returned to the printer. The pages she had run were now ready for proofreading. She tore them from the machine, removed the edges and put them in order. She would proofread them before going to bed.

As she picked up the pages she caught sight of herself in the slanted solarium glass. She wore a bright red turtleneck sweater and matching warm red tights. The red and green tartan shorts showed off her legs, which now, over four weeks after the cast had been removed, were both slender and straight. She pointed her foot before her like a ballerina, and then drew her newly healed leg in an elegant sweep around her. Turning sideways, she viewed herself. She didn't look half-bad, she thought. Her figure was slight, but nicely proportioned. With another careful flurry of arms and legs, she curtsied to her new image, and then picked up the papers, sat down on the chesterfield, and set to work.

She found it hard to concentrate and finally gave up. There was just too much else to think of tonight. It was over five weeks since she had had the new nightmare and almost as long since she had the cast removed, and in that time so much had happened. Stretching her legs out before her, she reflected that the very fast recovery of her leg was all due to Adam. She remembered the morning of the day she was to have the cast removed. Adam had marched her through his study and up to a door that she had often supposed led to a washroom. To her surprise, it led through a small exercise room to another door. Beyond this, she was astonished to see a swimming pool. She could tell from the atmosphere in the pool room that the water was heated and ready for use. Before she could begin to frame a question, Adam had turned to her, "Tell your doctor that you can swim every day. Get him to outline the kind of exercises that will help your leg. Try to get him to give you a printed sheet of them, then I can help you with them."

To say that she was stunned was to put it mildly. A pool here all this time and she had not known of its existence! As if reading her mind, Adam had explained, "I telephoned the Brownings and explained your situation. They were only too happy to know that we could make use of it."

But Lynn had hardly heard his explanation. Her attention had been riveted to his earlier remarks. Adam intended to help her exercise her leg? The thought had made her very uneasy.

To her dismay, it had all proved too true. That evening, after she had hobbled in on one good leg, one leg now free of a cast and a cane, Adam had insisted on reading the exercises. When he finished, he announced they would begin to work on the exercises the next morning and continue doing them twice a day until her leg had completely recovered. Lynn remembered thinking, that's all I need—Adam cracking the whip as I paddle up and down the pool in that skimpy green and blue bathing suit I purchased.

It had been even worse than she had imagined because when she had presented herself, primly wrapped up in a housecoat, Adam had been waiting, sleek and trim. Every muscle she had ever admired on Olympic divers was there in tantalizing clarity. They wove their way from his powerful shoulder and chest muscles to ripple enticingly down his abdomen and disappear beneath tight-fitting racing trunks. However, Adam had been supremely unconscious of his body and its affect on her.

Taking a sip from her coffee, she thought, the trouble was that crazy kiss. If he had never kissed her she would have continued on, oblivious to him. But ever since that fateful event she had grown increasingly aware of him. There was a certain tension she felt whenever they were together. If only she could remember. She must have had some experience with men. Instead she felt and acted like an adolescent.

Adam had slipped into the pool and like a sleek seal, quickly swum several laps, then he had stood up and approached the side of the pool. When she had just stood there, watching him totally mesmerized, he had held out his arms and said, "Hurry up. Get out of that dressing gown and sit down on the side of the pool. I'll lift you in and help you find out just what you are able to do."

Those words had caused another moment's panic. It had never crossed her mind that she might not know how to swim. But there was no time to stew about this because Adam was looking impatient. Hurriedly, she removed the robe, and with flaming face, carefully sat down on the side of the pool with the intention of slipping in. She should have known that she could not outwit Adam. Immediately she had been lifted by the waist and held suspended in the air, her feet dangling in the water. "You're as light as a feather," he had remarked as he carefully let her down until both feet were on the pool bottom. The water came up to her shoulders, and for a moment she felt swamped. As she stepped hesitantly forward, Adam explained, "The entire pool is the same depth. Ian Browning had the pool added when his wife had her stroke. He claimed that the daily exercise in it had more to do with the recovery of her mobility than anything else."

So they had begun the daily ritual that was to have her in a lather of shyness and embarrassment. At first Adam had tested her ability to swim, and she was relieved to discover that she could, however, not before Adam had insisted on holding her horizontal, and observed her ability to stroke and kick. She had been flustered by the firm grip he held on her waist. The taut, strong body so close to hers distracted her so much the first time that she had nearly submerged herself in a choking flurry of arms and legs. After that, she had settled down and learned the exercises. Soon, she had been able to do them herself to Adam's satisfaction. Instead of leaving, he would swim lengths while she worked on her leg. But all the time she had been unbearably aware of his long, slim, near-naked body with its powerful muscles that drove him through the water like some Greek god. She had hoped that when she could manage by herself Adam might go back to work, but he insisted that she never swim alone. In fact, he claimed that that had been the only condition the Brownings had made.

Lynn stretched out her legs, and poured herself another cup of coffee. The last month had been unusual for other reasons, too, she recalled. Not only had Adam worked her as hard as he did himself and still fit in the swimming exercises, he had also embarked on a series of interviews, speaking engagements and social events that took every spare moment he had. When she had questioned him about his suddenly busy calendar, he had explained that he had expected to be farther ahead with the book than he was and had allowed for some engagements in November. She now had the responsibility of organizing his time around these commitments, and she knew that there were more than he had initially planned because he had kept adding to the list. It was as if he was driven, she thought.

The most interesting appointments had been with the graduate students that he allowed to visit him. He had explained that his mentor, Ross Campbell, at Queen's University, had helped him a great deal with his postgraduate studies, and he felt it only right to agree to see his doctoral students. She remembered the strange case of the first student who was to come. Her name had been Sarah James, and they had waited patiently for her to show up. Adam had been annoyed when she had not arrived at the prescribed time and then concerned in case something had happened to her. That evening, he had telephoned the Dean of Economics at his home to discover if the young woman was ill. Lynn had only heard part of the conversation, but she picked up the fact that Adam was speaking to the Dean's wife, Shirley, whom he seemed to know on a first-name basis. Adam's voice had dropped then, so that she had not heard the rest of the conversation, but it had been short. Adam had come out of the study with a strange expression on his face. Lynn could not help asking, "What happened to her?"

She had been shocked when Adam said, "She's dead. She died late last summer, and no one realized that she had made this appointment. Shirley explained that it was a great loss, that the girl had probably been the most brilliant student that they had had in years. She said that Ross had been very broken up about it. However, she was fairly certain that the rest of the students would be coming as scheduled. If there was to be any change, Ross would get in touch."

The rest of the students had come, and Adam had encouraged her to sit in on these interviews. She had enjoyed these occasions. The students were enthusiastic and had interesting questions. The first of the three students had been a young man from British Columbia who had done all his predoctoral work at the University of British Columbia. Adam and he had hit it off right away since Adam had done his undergraduate work at UBC.

The second student had done his undergraduate work at Dalhousie in Nova Scotia, and had been equally keen, although the emphasis of his questions was on conservation and its effect on maritime economies.

But it had been the last student, Alain Marchant, who really captured Lynn's interest. He was a Québecois, and unlike the other students, he had done his master's degree at Queen's before beginning his doctoral program. His intelligence had been obvious, and as far as Lynn was concerned, he had asked the most insightful questions. It had been clear that Adam thought so too, because he asked him to stay for a drink after. Adam had switched into French sometime during the interview, and Lynn had followed the conversation without thought. It was only when Alain had risen to leave that it dawned on her that she must be fluent in French, and in particular, the Québecois idiom.

Alain had shaken hands with Adam and then turned to her. He had paused for a moment, a curious expression on his face. Then, with great charm, he had taken Lynn's hand and raised it to his lips. "It's a strange thing, Mademoiselle MacDougall," he had said, "All through this interview, I have had the feeling that I know you from somewhere. Alas, I am sure that I would have remembered such a lovely face. It has indeed been a pleasure meeting you."

Then, he had left, oblivious of the scowl that had appeared on Adam's face. Before Lynn had been able to discuss the interview with him, Adam had disappeared into his study, which was too bad, she thought, because she had had no opportunity to discuss her ability to speak French with him, and the occasion never seemed to arrive again.

With a sigh, Lynn poured out the last of the coffee.

And then she began rereading the pages, concentrating as hard as she could, but it was no use. In a short time her head settled against the back of the chesterfield, her eyes closed and the pages slipped from the fingers that held the pencil. The cup in her other hand sat cradled on her lap. She slept.

At two o'clock, Adam came home. Only the hall light was on so he assumed that Lynn had turned in. Wearily, he headed for the kitchen. Tonight he wanted a nightcap. He needed to unwind, to rid himself of the impatience he had experienced all evening. The last thing he had needed was another party. How had he let himself get sucked into this routine? Why?

The answer was all too obvious, he thought wryly. She was in that front room sleeping the sleep of the innocent while he was exhausting himself, night after night, trying to remove himself from temptation. It was that or fire her!

Strange, he thought. Lynn was anything but a temptress. She seemed the epitome of innocence, or at least she had been until he had made that fatal mistake and kissed her. Like lifting the lid of Pandora's box, the kiss had opened up feelings and tensions that he understood all too well, but he knew she only understood in part.

The swimming lessons had been dreadful. Every time he had lifted her into the pool it had been an effort to release her. He was sure that he had swum double the lengths just to keep down the frustration. And why did he have this protective streak where she was concerned? Ever since that first day in the hospital when she had so cleverly outwitted him, her frailty had stirred an allegiance he had never wanted or felt before. The words *a verray, parfit, gentle knyght* came to his mind. Well, he was no knight, no believer in ideal love. He didn't want to get caught in that trap of adolescent idealism. His intellectual interests and energies required that he be free to think and to work. He had no desire for those responsibilities that tied one to one place, limited one's experiences and restrained one's mind.

A little voice reminded him that with Lynn the intellectual spark was high-voltage. In no way did she cramp his thinking. In fact, even with her limited experience, she had developed the knack of challenging any fallacy in his reasoning.

Picking up his drink, he headed for the solarium. To his surprise, he saw that there was a light on her desk. Lynn must have finished the chapter and left it out for him, he thought, and looked for it on the desk, but it was not there. A small sound caught his attention, and he turned toward it. There, on the sofa, slept Lynn, curled up in the corner, one hand cradling a mug in a nest of scarlet tartan, one long red leg stretched out along the cushions, and the other, folded up beneath her. The pages of Chapter Two fanned down over the cushions and onto the floor.

Her presence startled Adam, and he stood, staring at her recumbent form, transfixed. At the sight of her, his heart had literally turned over. He felt as if he had been suddenly winded, and his hand trembled so that the ice in his drink rattled against the glass.

Now he knew why he had been running himself ragged in the social scene. He had been avoiding the truth, the truth that the slip of a girl sleeping before him was more important to him than he had ever thought possible. What he felt was so overpowering, so inclusive, that it could be nothing else but love. From the very beginning, he had been aware of her physically, even when he had known that she was unaware of him in that sense. He had grown to enjoy not only her company, but to look forward to the clarity of her thinking and the enthusiasm that she brought to her work. But now, somehow, it had all coalesced into something so much more. He wanted all of her—her passion, her spirit, her love.

It was all he could do to keep from bending down and kissing her awake, like the princess in the story, only he knew that she would never let him be her prince, not while her past remained hidden from her.

She sighed in her sleep, and eased her head on the sofa cushion. She was like some early Christmas surprise, he mused, in her green and scarlet shorts, red sweater and hose. The light glinted on her dark curls, and glowed softly on the pink of her cheeks. Her lashes lay curled against their satin, tempting him yet again and then she moved, trying to ease the leg that had been injured, and the mug teetered in her hand. Kneeling before her, he gently removed the mug, and the action woke her. Looking into his face, she smiled, and every resolution he had just made to keep his distance hovered on the brink of dissolution. He barely managed to smile in return, and say inanely, "It's late. You fell asleep reading the chapter."

Taking her hand, he helped her stand, and again she treated him to one of her smiles, and then, twirled around before him, and asked, "Do you like my outfit?"

"It's perfect," he assured her, and helped her pick

up the papers underfoot, and before he could weaken, urged her to turn in. Tonight he needed to be alone. He needed to think and to plan.

Lynn sat in a taxi with Adam headed for the Dunlops and wondered what on earth was going on. Adam had been rushing her about all day, and the activity had nothing to do with work. He had wakened her at eight that morning by knocking on the door and insisting that they go out for breakfast at the market. He had dragged her around the busy downtown farmer's market, examining the various stalls and produce and buying nothing. Then he had taken her to the Old Fish Market for breakfast. Not satisfied with that, he had then rushed them off to the Art Gallery of Ontario where they wandered aimlessly through one gallery after another. It had all been very pleasant, but completely pointless. And the whole time they were doing it, Lynn had had the feeling that Adam was following some secret agenda.

It was as if he had purposely chosen places guaranteed to be crowded with strangers, and at first she had been nervous until it became obvious to even her that no one was interested in her. The only really productive event of the day had been when they had visited the Henry Moore section at the Art Gallery. Just for a moment the place had been familiar. It was as if she had walked around that gallery with its wonderful large sculptures and open spaces before.

And now they were off to Tom's. It was quite a distance, and at first Adam had chatted about the art they had viewed, but as they got closer to his cousin's, he grew quiet, remote. Something was definitely on his mind. With a shrug, she settled back in the seat. One thing she had learned while working with Adam was that when he was in deep thought, as she humorously liked to call it, there was no point in trying to talk to him.

They were no sooner inside the Dunlops' door when Tom whisked Adam away to his study and Lynn joined Allison in the kitchen while she finished off the preparations for dinner.

Inside the study, Tom turned to Adam with a grin and asked, "What is so important that you can't discuss it with me on the telephone? Having trouble with your social calendar and need some medication for exhaustion? Or is it woman trouble?"

Even as the words left Tom's mouth, he realized that something was wrong. Adam was not smiling. He was standing tensely before him, his hands shoved in his trouser pockets. Tom waited.

Finally, Adam spoke. "I have a problem, Tom, and I need your help."

"What kind of help?"

"I want to help Lynn get back her memory, and I want to do it as soon as possible. I want you to see if you can get me a copy of the records made about her when she arrived at the hospital, and a copy of the information that the police gave you about her."

Tom could not hide his surprise or his concern. "Come on, Adam. That stuff is confidential. The only person that has any right to see the medical records is Lynn herself. And I'm not sure that they would tell either of you anything that you did not already know. Why this sudden need to know about her?"

He watched as Adam picked up a book on his desk

and weighed it in his hand. Finally, as if having come to some important decision, he put it down and looked up at Tom. "I've fallen in love with her, and I know that I don't have a hope with her until she remembers who she is."

If it had not been for the serious expression on Adam's face, Tom would have burst into laughter. His tall, handsome, clever cousin had finally been caught. He remembered how Adam had shaken his head when Tom had told him he was getting married, and said, "Better you than me." And here he was, before him, actually blushing, because he knew darn well what Tom was thinking. "Does she love you?"

Adam walked around the room, rubbing the back of his neck, and finally turned and said, "I don't think so. So far, our relationship has been that of employer and employee. That is, until today. Today I began a plan to change that relationship. But even if she did love me, she would not admit to it. I know how her mind works. She thinks something dreadful happened to her, and she would be afraid of involving someone she loved. In fact, today at the Art Gallery, I'm sure that she remembered something. Just for a moment, she seemed lost in a trance. Then she turned away and acted as if nothing had happened."

"What do you mean that you began a plan to change your relationship, Adam?"

"I intend to . . . er . . . court her."

Again Tom wanted to explode with laughter, but the light in Adam's eye warned him that he had better not. Adam *court* a girl. Adam, the lover of two continents, gorgeous women all over the place, *courting* a girl. It was too good to be true and not fair that he was not being allowed to tease him.

Finally, Adam admitted, "All right, Tom, I know what you're thinking, and you are right. The last thing I ever thought you would hear me say was that I was in love, or that I wanted to court somebody. You told me that when it happened to me I would not have any choice in the matter. You were right. So you see that it is really important I get all the information possible to try to solve this mystery. Then Lynn will be free to consider any feelings she might have for me."

Tom considered Adam's request seriously, and finally said, "I cannot let you see her medical records, but I will do this for you. I will get all the records I can legally examine and reread them. If I find any details that I think might help, I'll tell you about them. Why don't you go to the police?"

"That's the one thing I don't want to do just now. It's obvious that whoever hurt Lynn lost track of her or thinks she is dead. If I started talking to the police, their interest might alert her enemy. For now, I want to examine any information you can get. Also, I intend to read copies of the newspapers around the time of the accident. Maybe I'll pick up a clue there. If I have to, I'll go to Ottawa to see her last employer, but again, I'm not keen to do this in case I alert someone. Look, let me know as soon as you have found out anything. Anything! Even something as insignificant as what she was wearing."

When Adam and Tom finally came out, Lynn and Allison were playing a game with the two children on the living-room floor. Whatever Adam's problem had been, Lynn thought, he seemed to have solved it.

Over supper, however, she became aware that Tom was watching her. And when they all gave a hand in cleaning up, he asked how she was enjoying her job. When she told him that it was the best thing that had ever happened to her, he seemed satisfied.

When they returned home that night, Adam was much more relaxed than when they had traveled to the Dunlops, and as they entered the house they discussed the board game the four of them had played that evening. But, after handing Adam her jacket to hang up, Lynn decided she needed answers. She turned to him and asked, "Why did you break our regular routine today, Adam? Why the trip to the market and the Art Gallery?"

She watched him carefully as he turned from hanging up her jacket. Quite unexpectedly, he reached out and touched her cheek. "I just wanted to enjoy a day with you without the stress of work. Was that so terrible?"

She felt herself color at the touch of his hand, and was unable to form a response. *He wanted to enjoy a day with her.* The thought sent a glow through her.

He continued to watch her, those gray eyes with their yellow lights alert, probing. "Did you enjoy yourself?"

She considered the day for a moment and then she smiled. "Of course I did. At least, I did when I realized that no one seemed to recognize me, that it was safe. I guess this face is a pretty good mask to hide behind."

She didn't know just how revealing her words

were but Adam picked up their significance immediately. Lynn still did not associate herself with the
lovely face that looked at him. Somewhere in her
subconscious, her forgotten self was hiding, staring
out through the features that she denied. What would
happen, he wondered, when that self felt safe
enough to risk discovery?

However, there was no solution to that problem
right now, and Adam had another item on his
agenda to deal with. While he still had her cornered,
so to speak, in the hallway where he could watch
her reactions, he asked, "Since you felt safe enough
today, do you think you could risk attending a party
with me next Saturday? I would be honored if you
would be my date."

His date, Lynn thought wildly. *Date* had so many
connotations. If he had said companion, she would
not have had any problem, but *date!*

Adam watched the emotions flick across her face.
He knew he had risked a lot using the word "date,"
but he wanted to change their relationship, and
change it quickly.

"Come on, Lynn, you'll have fun. This is the
newspaper crowd. The business editor of *The Globe*
is having a small party. You'll enjoy meeting the
other guests. Most of them you know of anyway.
And I'll fill you in on their backgrounds so that you
feel comfortable. You'll find the group stimulating,
and I promise, I won't leave you alone for a minute."

She looked at Adam, panic in her eyes. Panic not
only caused by the idea of dating, but also by the
idea of meeting new people, and not just anyone, but

clever, astute ones, "I don't know about this, Adam,
I . . . ' '

He started to walk toward the kitchen, then turned
to her as she followed. "Come on, admit it. You're
going stir-crazy. You're ready to break out. Why do
you think you bought all those new clothes?"

Was she? Was that why she had shopped so
much? Was she ready to begin the search? For in
actual fact, regardless of what agenda Adam had,
hers would be to watch for any clue that could lead
to her forgotten past.

Adam was nothing if not pleased with himself the
next day when he climbed into a taxi and headed
downtown to the Toronto Reference Library. He had
won his gamble about the date. For whatever reason,
Lynn had decided to go along with the idea. All
morning, they worked at full speed on the third
chapter of his book, and he left her with piles of
notes to enter on the word processor. It was amazing. Over the weeks they had developed a kind of
personal shorthand between them. He could sketch
out his idea in pencil, and she would enter it in
prose that was every bit as good as his. He did not
like to do this all the time, but right now he had two
priorities demanding his time, the book and Lynn's
mystery.

When he reached the library, he asked for the
microfiche copies of the major Toronto papers for
the weeks covering the time of Lynn's accident. The
details were quite horrifying. A car had had a blow-
out that caused it to swerve into the neighboring
lane. In an effort to avoid the car, a transport had

jackknifed and the bus behind had collided with it. A car traveling behind the bus had driven into the back of the bus, and it was this event that made what was already a very serious set of accidents into a tragedy. Miraculously, people were injured by the first events, but not seriously. But the last car exploded a few minutes after the collision before everyone on the bus had been freed. One article actually mentioned Lynn as being the last person to be rescued from the bus before the explosion. One other person, who it seemed had been trapped in the bus's washroom at the moment of collision, had died in the explosion and resulting fire.

As Adam read on in the next day's news, lists of the survivors were published, and horrendous pictures showed the devastation. Over the next few days, all news of the accident disappeared except for the mention of the fact that so far the authorities had been unable to identify the person in the washroom. Other than stating that the person had been a woman, no other evidence was available due to the tremendous heat of the fire. No one came forward to claim a lost friend or relative. Very soon, any mention of the unknown person disappeared out of the papers altogether.

Adam was just about to remove the film from the projector when the name of his alma mater, Queen's University, caught his eye. He paused to read the article which had merited a large headline on the front page—QUEEN'S STUDENT MISSING. With a sigh, Adam pondered the state of the world when young women were not safe. His perusal of the article was casual until the phrase "brilliant doctoral student in economics'' caught his eye. Remembering the student who had failed to come to the interview, he re-read the article carefully. Sure enough. The student was Sarah James.

Adam read on. Sarah, it seemed, was the third young woman who had disappeared in the last year. Unfortunately, the bodies of the first two young women had been found, but there was no news of Sarah. It seemed that when she had not returned to the university in September to take up her position as teaching assistant and doctoral student, the dean of her faculty had notified the police. They were trying to reach a stepbrother who it seemed was away on a hunting trip.

Adam flicked on over the next few days of the paper, but there was no more news, just a repetition of what he already knew, that she was missing.

Adam remembered clearly that the Dean's wife had told him on the telephone that Sarah James was dead. The thought of such talent being wasted caused him to continue his search. No new information appeared in the microfiche he had, so he returned it and exchanged it for the next month's editions. Sitting down again, he searched for any more mention of the student. Then he saw it. Several weeks after her disappearance, Sarah's car had been found in a remote area, and there was evidence of foul play. There were minute spots of blood in the trunk, and several very long strands of her hair. Police assumed that she had met the same fate as the other young women. By then, a relative had been located, a stepbrother, who said that he had been unaware that Sarah had disappeared. He had been away in an area northwest of Ottawa on a fishing expedition. He had explained that they had very little to do with each other and that he had not seen her in over a year. Adam wondered how he had missed seeing the article at the time. Too busy working on his book, he supposed.

Adam sat there, deep in thought. Maybe he was grasping at straws, maybe not. But it was just possible that he had discovered Lynn's identity. It would explain so much, her knowledge of economics, and the marks of restraint on her wrists and ankles. It would also explain why her subconscious was trying to protect her. Someone out there had tried to murder her, and had not succeeded. If she was to remember and name the person she would be at risk.

But maybe he was just looking for miracles. Maybe this poor girl was dead. How to proceed?

The first logical step would be to go to Kingston and talk to Ross Campbell. However, he thought, if I do that, I would immediately be involving the police, because Ross, as Dean, would have to notify them of my suspicions. Then he remembered Alain Marchant. Alain would have been a master's student at Queen's when Sarah was there. They must have been in most of the same classes. He had been impressed by Alain, and was sure he would keep what he was told to himself. Well, he decided, it was something that he had to risk. He thought about his schedule for the next few days. He would find a way to clear enough time to drive down to Kingston and see him.

*   *   *

Lynn sat back from the pile of work that Adam had left her. It was time she took a break. Standing and stretching, she walked over to the solarium glass. During the night there had been a light fall of snow, and it still clung to the bushes. Chickadees hopped about their branches, causing miniature snowfalls as they searched among the branches for seeds and grubs. In one of the high trees beyond, a male cardinal, glorious in red feathers, cleaned his back on a branch and then flashed away. She wondered if they could get a bird-feeder. If they were going to be there all winter, surely the Brownings would not mind.

Well, she mused, the die is cast. I'm committed at last to going out with Adam. I don't know which I am more afraid of, the risk of finding out something about myself, or the idea of being Adam's date. Things seemed to be shifting between them. All morning she had been unusually aware of him. At moments, she would lose track of what they were doing because she found herself watching him, noting the fine bones of his face, the way his hair clung to the shape of his skull, the lithe movements he made as he made a point or moved around the room. And she was aware that he was watching her in a way that he had never done before. What a pain in the neck it was not to remember, she thought with frustration. Surely she must have been more experienced than she felt. Maybe that was why every time that morning when she thought she would decline the date, something stopped her. Maybe she had had enough of leading a shadow life that belonged only to the present and the pretty face that greeted her each day.

The ringing of the telephone interrupted her thoughts, and she turned to her desk to answer it, expecting Adam. Instead, she heard a woman's voice. It seemed to be that of an older woman, and she thought it might be Adam's mother. However, when she asked, it turned out to be Marion Browning who explained that Adam had called them on their ship, but that they had been away overnight on the island of Fiji and had only now gotten the message.

After Lynn explained that Adam was out, she took the opportunity to thank Marion Browning for the use of their pool. Marion was a charming person, and eager to share the experiences she had had in the pool while recovering from her stroke. Then, Lynn remembered the picture in her room. She had always wanted to find out more about Martine Hébért. For some reason, it seemed important. So, gathering her courage, she asked Marion if she knew anything about her.

Marion was full of the story. She had purchased the picture about a year before the artist had died. It seemed that Martine Hébért had grown up in Quebec, but had taken her degree in Fine Arts in Ontario at Queen's. She had settled in Kingston after that and had become a popular local artist. Marion had seen her work and purchased her picture at a show while holidaying on the nearby Thousand Islands in the St. Lawrence River. The following year she had been saddened to hear that the young artist had died of cancer. Her pictures were highly valued now, and Marion felt that she was most fortunate to have one. It was with a sinking heart that Lynn had finished the conversation. In the back of her mind, she had hoped that the sense of familiarity she felt for the painting might have been a clue, but if the artist was dead, then there was nothing to pursue. Depressed, she went back to her desk. At least when she was working she could forget her troubles, and she settled down for another stint at the word processor.

Lynn had her hair cut and styled Saturday. Returning home, she hurried to her room to have another look at herself. She realized finally that she was becoming comfortable with the face in the mirror, more at one with it. Her hair had been trimmed considerably, and curled around her face, down her neck and around her ears. Looking at the style with a hand-mirror, she decided that the cut set off the shape of her head, and emphasized the length of her neck. The series of thoughts caused her to frown at herself with alarm. Was this face of hers making her vain?

Well, she thought, I hope not. Anyway, I need this face to keep me safe tonight. I need to feel confident about myself.

At supper, Adam gently teased her when she came in, obviously self-conscious about her hair. ''Well, well, well. New hair style, eh? Heavy date tonight? Somebody's a lucky guy.''

She relaxed with the teasing and strutted around, her nose in the air. ''You'd better believe it. It was done by the salon's top stylist, and cost an arm and a leg.''

They kept up this banter all through supper, and Adam felt more at ease with his conscience when he realized that she really was enjoying herself and looking forward to the evening.

Even though he had seen her newly styled hair at supper, he was not prepared for the full impact she had on him when she presented herself in the living room later. She wore a dress of rich cranberry red. The long-sleeved dress draped gently over her shoulders and was nipped in at the waist by a subtly worked fabric belt. The skirt flared out to swirl seductively at him as she turned shyly before him and waited for his approval.

Dampening down the urge to kneel before her and confess every honorable and dishonorable thought he had, he took her hand, touched it with his lips and murmured, ''I was right, mademoiselle, you're date is a very luck man,'' and taking her arm, he led her to the hall. As he helped her on with her coat, and insisted she wear her snow boots, at least until they arrived at the party, he fought down the urge to tell her how he felt, and live with the consequences. But then he caught her expression. He saw the bravado and fear in her eyes, and remembered his plan. Before she could change her mind, he rushed her out to the waiting cab.

The party was held in the west part of Toronto known as the Kingsway. The homes were older but large and welcoming, and when they stepped into the hallway of the house, she immediately relaxed. Here was a house that, regardless of the exclusive nature of the guests expected, was also a home where children resided. In a large hallway, two bicycles stood under an array of ski jackets and were surrounded by running shoes. Their host, a balding man in his forties, apologetically explained that the guests' coats must be taken upstairs to one of the bedrooms. Lynn was interested to see two teenage boys poring over a computer in what seemed to be their father's study. Another bedroom was obviously that of a young girl, with attractive floral curtains and bedspread, and a bevy of stuffed animals. The homey flavor of the scene caused the tension that had been growing in her to uncoil, and she turned and smiled at Adam, causing his heart to turn over with happiness. He had not been wrong to risk a party at Richard's. Erudite as the guests might be, the setting was right for Lynn's first foray into society. Taking her hand, he led her downstairs and into a fairly crowded living room where people were gathering for drinks and hors d'oeuvres. Keeping his arm around her waist and making it clear that she was with him, he proceeded to introduce her to the people present.

Many of the guests were people whose articles she had read in *Maclean's, Saturday Night, The Globe & Mail, The Sun* and *The Star.* There was even a well-known television economist and her husband. After a few minutes, Lynn realized this was a rather close-knit community with almost everyone knowing someone else, and that Adam seemed to be the reason for them all being there, the guest of honor. Even the elegant blond journalist she had seen on the television news was present. Dressed in the perfect clinging little black dress, long legs accented by glitter-trimmed hose, a young woman glided across the room toward Adam. Bemused, Lynn found herself being introduced to her as his friend and associate, and was fascinated to see the young woman, Jean, back off.

Adam led her through to another room, a large family room where some of the guests had already settled into small groups to talk animatedly about everything from the latest play in town to that day's value of the Canadian dollar. Instead of being threatened by the people present, Lynn found herself quietly enjoying their conversation. No one seemed to question her presence. Instead, they seemed to accept that because Adam was beside her, she had every right to be there.

Sometime later, they moved off toward the living room again to refresh their drinks when a voice rang out, "Adam, *mon chér, comment ça va?*" They both turned to see a tall, long-legged beauty coming toward them. A swath of golden hair rippled around the shoulders of one of the most beautiful women Lynn had ever seen. She had to be French, thought Lynn. Only a Frenchwoman could enter a room with such confidence and dress with such chic. When she reached Adam, she seemed about to throw herself in his arms, but Adam neatly managed to switch the embrace into a very proper European greeting, a kiss on either cheek. Then, before the woman could say anything, he said, "Andrée. How wonderful to see you again. You look great, as usual. What takeover brought you to this side of the Atlantic?"

It was obvious to Lynn that this was not quite

how Andrée had anticipated this conversation to go. Ignoring his question, she smiled beguilingly, and said, "As soon as James," and she gestured to a man standing behind her, "said that you were coming tonight, I insisted that he bring me. I've missed you so much. Life hasn't been the same since Greece."

Boy, thought Lynn sourly. How was it possible to say the word *Greece*, and imply so much more? But Adam ignored the insinuation, and reached past her to shake James's hand. "Hello, James. Good to see you again. It's been three years, hasn't it? I think I ran into you when the Group of Seven met. Seems to me that we had quite a night on the town as I remember." Then, without a pause, he put his arm around Lynn, and said, "I would like you to meet Lynn MacDougall, a close friend and the best research assistant that I have ever had." Handshakes were exchanged, and as Lynn and the blond surreptitiously sized each other up, and James looked with open admiration at her, Adam cleverly led the conversation toward the latest economic crisis in Europe. The entire time, he kept his arm possessively on her waist.

Somewhere deep within Lynn an imp of mischief began to burble up and overcome first her jab of jealousy at the blond's obvious interest in Adam and, second, her confusion over Adam's close proximity to her and the fact that he seemed to be saying very clearly to James, "Hands off, Buster, she's mine." It was all beginning to have the elements of a French farce, she thought. She's sending out messages to Adam, James is leering at me, and Adam is playing the heavy-handed lover.

It was a relief when their host and hostess invited them to help themselves to a lavish buffet set up in a very elegant dining room. Again, Adam kept her by his side, steering them away from the eager Andrée. When they had filled their plates, he led her to a comfortable chair in the living room and pulled a nearby footstool up close to the chair. Sitting on the stool, he inquired quietly if she would like to put up her injured leg. Nothing gets by him, she thought. He knows darn well that I should not have worn these silly shoes, and he's noticed me shifting my weight off my leg. However, she answered equally quietly, "No. You stay on the stool. My leg will be fine if I keep it out straight." She should have known that nothing she said would deter him when he got an idea. With a glint in his eye that dared her to make an issue of what he was about to do, he lifted her leg up and placed it close beside him on the stool. Too close, as far as she was concerned. As he turned to enter the conversation that was going on within the cluster of people around them sitting on the sofa and chairs, he settled against her. Another statement of intimacy that quite confused her.

The group of people they had joined were in the middle of an interesting conversation, and soon both she and Adam were drawn into it. They were discussing an act of shocking violence that had occurred on the streets of Toronto just the day before. Their host was sitting with them, and he began to wonder out loud about the nature of evil, and whether such an incident was an example of evil.

There ensued a very lively discussion as to what kind of act was evil and what was simply an act without forethought. Members of the group began considering actions that they thought might be considered truly evil. Was the crazed behavior of a psychopath evil? How did that compare to a sane person who killed without compunction? Were there other kinds of evil? In the very vocal crowd, everyone had an opinion. While they were talking, Adam's reporter friend, Jean, joined the group and like everyone, had an opinion. Lynn listened to this discussion, fascinated by both the subject and the interesting views being exchanged. She was surprised, however, when Jean suddenly turned to Lynn and said, "Ms. MacDougall, you've been very quiet about this. What kind of person do you think is evil?"

Lynn knew that she was being baited, and she could feel Adam tensing, ready to leap to her defense. However, while she had been listening she had been thinking about that very question, and found that she had an answer ready. "I think that an evil person is one who has no compassion. One who uses every opportunity to fulfill his own desires without feeling or conscience, regardless of the harm he does to others. I think such a person is always driven by his own needs, be they ambition, greed or physical desire." Even as she spoke, a persona seemed to drift into her consciousness. For just a moment, she felt that she was describing someone. She could almost feel a presence and see a face. On the word *greed*, she could hear her voice waver for a second, and she needed to pause and gain control of it. She managed to finish her statement, but she wondered what it was that had triggered that feeling, and she felt quite shattered. Fatalistically she could see Jean watching her like a hawk, ready to zero in on her statement. The sudden toppling over of some carelessly piled-up china on the coffee table interrupted the conversation, and gave Lynn an opportunity to escape. She rescued some of the dishes along with another guest, and headed for the kitchen.

The man who had also sprung up to save the china helped her place the dishes on the kitchen counter, and introduced himself as Al. He was just about to engage her in a conversation when Jean entered with some dishes also. I should have known she would follow me, Lynn thought. She wants to know about me because of Adam, and she has a reporter's nose. A dangerous combination.

Sure enough. The reporter turned and asked, "Have you known Adam for long?"

Lynn busied herself with tidying dishes that did not need rearranging as she answered, "I've known him since September when I started working for him. He did tell you that I was his assistant?"

Al looked annoyed at having his conversation interrupted, but Jean was too clever to let him get a word in edgewise. "Just what do you do as an assistant?"

Lynn looked at her levelly, not missing the innuendo behind the remark. "I put his manuscript on the word processor as he completes each section."

"Oh, you're a clerk-typist?"

Catty, thought Lynn, and answered, "I also do research for him."

"I notice you limp," continued Jean, obviously not giving up the attack. "What happened to your leg?"

"What are you doing, Jean?" Adam's stern voice interrupted. "Trying to make a news story of Lynn? Let me give you some facts. She is the best assistant I have ever had. She is also the most beautiful. And, like myself, she values her privacy. Go ply your trade somewhere else."

Lynn could have sagged with relief when she heard his voice, and could not help but smile her welcome to him. He smiled back, put the ever-protective arm around her shoulders, and led her back to the dining room for dessert. They returned to the chair and stool they had left, and spent the rest of the evening with the others. Jean had received the message and took herself elsewhere.

As they were getting ready to leave, their hostess approached Adam. "I wondered, Adam, if anyone has tried to sell you tickets to the fund-raiser for the Toronto Sick Children's Hospital. It's being held in the Winter Garden Theater. First, you see a preview of a Noël Coward revival that opens the next night. Then there is a buffet and a dance held in the lobby of the theater. It's quite the most important charity event of the year, and terribly expensive, but for a good cause. It's a week from Saturday. Black tie and all that. I would be honored if both of you would consider coming and sharing our table. Think about it and let me know."

Adam almost accepted on the spot, but caution stopped him, and he smiled at his charming hostess. "I'll check our schedule and let you know tomorrow."

And as he helped Lynn with her coat and into the waiting taxi, he was already working out a plan to ensure that they both attended.

All in all, she thought as they drove home in the taxi, it had been a very nice party. Although she had not been one of the professionals who had been very busy networking as well as socializing, she had enjoyed their company and felt at ease with them. Except for Jean and Andrée.

They talked quietly about nothing in particular as they traveled home; the fact that it had snowed a little, that people were getting out their outdoor Christmas lights. Inconsequential things. It was not until they had reached the house and were standing in the hall as Adam hung up their coats that he asked her if she had had a good time at the party. "I enjoyed it," she said honestly. "I didn't expect to, but I did. They were all very kind to me. They all seemed to know each other, and yet they included me in their discussions. All, except Jean, of course. I had the feeling that her news-woman's nose was twitching for a story."

He smiled down at her and assured her, "You don't have to worry about Jean." And then, without warning, he reached out and caressed her face. "I had a good time tonight. I was proud to be with you." At these words, Lynn's heart gave a lurch, and the sensation of his hand along her cheek stopped the breath in her throat. "I watched you all night, so lovely in your red dress, your hair shimmering in the light, your eyes lighting up with interest at the conversation, and I wanted to do this." And his hand slipped behind her head and drew her toward him. She watched him, as he lowered his head toward her. Watched his mouth until she was forced to close her eyes, and then felt his lips contact. As they moved across hers, she felt herself sinking beneath a wash of pleasure so great that with a sigh she collapsed against him, lost on the flame of his kiss. He tightened his hold, and deepened the kiss, and she found herself slowly responding. It was he who finally ended it, holding her head against his shoulder, and giving her a minute to steady herself. He seemed to realize how shattered she was, how new this was to her, for he rubbed his cheek against her hair and whispered, "You need never worry about the likes of Jean, or indeed, Andrée. You are all that I could ever want in a woman. And now, I think that you had better go to bed before my best intentions disappear, and I earn the wrath of my estimable cousin who has trusted me with your virtue as well as your safety." He kissed her softly on the forehead this time, turned her gently away, and watched as she tried with some degree of composure to walk across the living room to her room.

Lynn closed her door in a trance and walked toward the washroom. Turning on the light, she stood and stared at herself. But the face she saw in no way reflected the confusion she felt, or the reaction of her body to Adam's kiss. It throbbed in ways she had never suspected possible. She touched her lips and blushed as she remembered her avid response. And then she recalled the words, *You are all that I could ever want in a woman.* What had he meant by that exactly? And more important, what did she want it to mean?

In the darkened solarium, Adam stood staring out into the night. A gentle snow fell on the scene, but he did not see it. I just couldn't keep my hands off her, he fumed. Now I have probably frightened her away. I am supposed to be winning her affection, not swamping her with my own need. He hit one of the cedar arches in disgust. Yet she responded gloriously to my kisses, he thought, and left me aching for more.

Tomorrow he would have to do better. He would try to reach Alain, and he had promised Tom that he would come over and discuss what Tom had found in the records. He had a horrible feeling that his cousin was going to want him to stop. Well, it would be up to him to convince him otherwise.

Standing in Tom's study early the next morning, reading through the notes Tom had given him, Adam had to admit that his cousin was nothing if not thorough. When he finished, Tom said, "Take my word for it, Adam. There is nothing in the files that will tell you anything new. The only thing that can be said is that Lynn must have the best luck on record. It's hard to understand why she didn't have a broken neck as well as a broken jaw after reading that dreadful accident report." Tom paused and looked uncomfortable. "I've been thinking about it, Adam, and I don't think you have the right to pursue this without Lynn's approval. I remember clearly, at Thanksgiving, that she said she wanted to wait until she felt completely sure of herself before trying to discover any answers."

Adam watched his cousin as he spoke. He could see the stubborn look that he had known as a child cross Tom's face. When Tom made up his mind, it was very hard to change it. With a sigh, he realized that if he wanted his cooperation he would have to tell him everything. And *everything* was just so much speculation.

Putting the papers down on Tom's desk, he walked to the window, and tried to choose the right words. Finally, he turned and said, "I think I know who Lynn is."

"You what?"

"I said that I think I know who Lynn is. And better still, I think that I can convince you that I'm right!"

Returning to the desk, he picked up an envelope he had brought with him and said, "Come on over here and sit down, and take a look at the evidence."

For once in his life, Adam thought with amusement, Tom was speechless. He came over to the desk, pulled up a chair, and waited.

Adam pulled out Xeroxed copies of newspaper articles and handed them to him. "I first tried to find out all that I could about the accident, and like you, found nothing new. I was just about to give up when I noticed a headline on one of the microfiche projections. It was this." And he handed Tom a copy of the article about the missing Queen's student. He then handed him a series of follow-up articles that chronicled the history of the lost girl, and waited while he read them.

When Tom had finished, he turned to Adam and said, "You think that Sarah James is Lynn?"

"Why not?" challenged Adam. "The information all fits. I know that there are no pictures of the girl in the paper, something that is odd and needs to be looked into, however, there is a physical description here,'' and he pointed to some highlighted lines in one of the articles. *"She was five feet four inches, was a brunette and had blue eyes.* Even the problem with her jaw was explained. Also, it says she was a remarkable economics student. The word used over and over to describe her talents is 'brilliant.' It would seem that she had no immediate family, which would explain why no one was looking for her, although I find the behavior of the stepbrother somewhat suspicious.'' Adam then waited while Tom read over all the articles again and sat back in thought.

"It's uncanny, isn't it? What amazes me is that I didn't notice these articles.'' Checking the dates on the stories, Tom went on, "I suppose the reason I didn't make the connection is that these articles begin on September sixth when it was realized that Lynn was missing, and I worked on her in the middle of August. Have you shown these to Lynn?''

"No. There are a number of things I want to check out first. I think that I need to be very sure before I discuss this with her. Now you know why I want to proceed, and why I want your blessing.''

Tom sat for a long time, obviously weighing up the pros and cons. "There is a risk here, you know. You could put Lynn in danger with your poking around.''

"I know,'' replied Adam. "That's why I would like to go over the steps I intend to take with you and get any suggestions you might have.''

"Okay. You've got my help.''

At those words, Adam walked around the room. His relief was overwhelming. His hand shook as he ran it through his hair in an effort to ease his tension. In a strained voice, he turned to Tom and said, "Thank you. I can't tell you how much this means. She is becoming as important as breath itself to me. I can't imagine life without her anymore. Crazy, isn't it."

Then, pulling out the chair, he sat down beside Tom and mapped out a plan of action he had made. He explained about Alain Marchant, and they both agreed that if after the interview he felt Alain was trustworthy, he should share his secret with him if it seemed prudent. Together they studied the articles, discussing each fact. The more they read, the more they disliked the cold fish of a stepbrother who managed not to be around and who claimed little knowledge of the girl. When Adam said, "I wish I knew a good detective," Tom grinned and picked up the telephone book. "I just might be able to help you here."

With a mysterious smile, he located a number, made a note of it, and then explained, "I went through premeds with a guy who decided that he was not cut out for medicine and changed to law. He's a brilliant criminal lawyer now. I'll give him a call and see if he can recommend a detective. Certainly he would need one in his business."

Adam went out to see if Allison had some coffee on the burner. By the time he returned, coffee mugs in hand, Tom had completed his call. "I have just the man. He is the owner of Bowers Investigation. George says that Sam Bowers was a well-thought-of detective on the Metropolitan Toronto Police Force, but that a few years ago his wife took very ill, and since he had a young family, he found he could not look after the kids, visit his wife in the hospital and work a police-man's hours, too. He retired and set up his own busi-ness. George says that it is the best thing he ever did. He has developed a team that is honest, efficient and discreet. Another advantage is that Sam has kept a good working relationship with the police, and con-sequently gets their cooperation when he needs back-ground on a suspected felon. Here's his number. He suggested that we telephone him tomorrow as he tries very hard to keep his weekends free. Sadly, his wife died of her illness.''

By the time Adam left, they had agreed on a com-plete list of things that Adam should do, and as Adam drove home, he felt as if a huge weight had been re-moved from his shoulders. His cousin's approval lifted his spirits, and the feeling that he was doing something correctly had him humming along with an early Christmas carol on the car radio. There and then, he vowed that he would solve Lynn's mystery before Christmas.

Lynn slept late after the party. When she had dressed, she headed for the kitchen. She hoped that Adam had eaten and was locked up in his study. She was not sure just how she was going to cope with him after her behavior of the night before. And his behav-ior, too, she thought. However, she need not have wor-ried. There was no sight of Adam. Instead there was a paper standing against a coffee mug on the counter with the message: *Had to go out. Will be back soon.* That certainly doesn't tell me much, she thought. *De-cide where in the solarium you would like to put the Christmas tree.*

The Christmas tree! It's only the end of November, she thought. Surely Adam is rushing things a bit. But then, the idea of having their own tree warmed her imagination. It would make it seem just like a home; as if she belonged here. Humming a carol to herself, she made her breakfast, then hurried to the solarium to choose just the right space. By the time she had decided, Adam was at the front door calling for her assistance. When she hurried to the front hall, she was amazed to see Adam putting down the second set of two pots of flowers. ''Move these away from the door, and be ready to get some more,'' he called. *More,* she thought. Has he gone crazy? She carried down no less than fourteen paper-covered pots before she had finished, and was bent down peeking into the wrappers to see what kind of plant was hidden underneath, when Adam joined her.

''Poinsettias,'' he grinned. ''What house is complete without poinsettias at Christmas? Come on. Help me carry them into the solarium. I thought we could bank them in groups against the windows. And then we can put up the tree.''

He picked up a couple of the pots and headed for the solarium. ''There,'' he stopped and grinned, ''I just love Christmas, and I haven't had a Canadian one for three years. Come on, hurry up!''

Several hours later, Lynn sat down on the solarium chesterfield in bemusement. In the late November dusk, a large artificial fir tree twinkled with a multitude of little fairy lights. They were reflected in countless shiny colored globes and glass icicles that hung from the tree's branches. Glittering chains looped around it. Red, pink and white poinsettias were grouped along the windows, adding to the ambience. Adam had even found a compact disc of carols in the Brownings' collection, and its sound floated through the house as they worked. To Lynn's surprise, Adam had a fine baritone voice. He hummed the harmonies of all the pieces on the disc, When Lynn remarked on this, Adam explained that both Tom and he had sung as youngsters in a children's choir in a downtown church. When Lynn joked about the very idea of Tom and Adam being good long enough to learn to sing, Adam was quick to correct her. "They had a remarkable organist and choir leader. He inspired us to sing. At Christmas, he told us that we could sing carols with the angels, and in that wonderful old church, it felt like it. Tom and his family still attend the church, and the children sing in the junior choir. We'll have to go to the carol service at Christmas."

Adam made a tray of tea and brought it in. Pouring out the tea, he handed her a cup and picking up his, said, "Here's to the very best Christmas possible, Lynn. May all your Christmas wishes come true."

In the soft light of the tree, she studied his face. When had it become so dear to her? she wondered. And she realized that she wished he could be part of all her Christmases, impossible as it seemed. Sometime soon, her memory would return, and she would have to put her two lives together. Adam would finish his book and return to his former life of roaming consultant. But for now, she decided with determination, she intended to enjoy what she had and be grateful for it.

Adam, watching her expressive face, observed her pleasure as she viewed their afternoon's work, and her sadness as she thought of her future. Hoping to distract her with yet another item in his campaign, he asked, "Do you think that you and I could cook a Christmas turkey? I have spoken to the Brownings, and they said that we were welcome to use their dining room. I thought that we could invite Tom, Allison and the kids for Christmas dinner. What do you think?"

And even as she agreed enthusiastically that yes she was sure that they could cook a turkey, she worried that this all seemed too good to be true, and the feeling of belonging, of being a part of something, could disappear as quickly as one could pull out the Christmas lights glittering before her.

Adam leaned back against the wall of the elevator that was taking him to the sixth floor of the downtown Victorian building in which Sam Bowers's offices were situated. He glanced at his watch. Only ten o'clock. He already felt confidence in the investigator who had returned his eight o'clock recorded message almost instantly, and set up a meeting with him at the earliest possible hour. The man's style on the telephone had added to his sense that things would turn out all right, that using a detective was a correct move.

Things were perking along with his other campaign, too. He had convinced Lynn that she should accompany him to the charity benefit at The Winter Garden. Mind you, it had taken some conniving. Remembering that as a child while staying with Tom's parents he had had to be rushed to Sick Kids with a bizarre virus, he had built the incident up a little, and won over Lynn's soft heart. She had agreed that it was very

necessary that Adam should attend any function that
would profit such a wonderful institution, and, with
some hesitation, had agreed to go with him.

The elevator reached the sixth floor and opened on
to a very tasteful reception area of dark mahogany.
After introducing himself to the receptionist, he was
led into Sam Bowers's office.

Sam Bowers was a tall, well-built man with close-
cropped graying hair, alert brown eyes, and magnificent carriage. When he moved across the office to
greet Adam and lead him to a seat, Adam was more
aware of his intelligent scrutiny than of his size and
movement. Sam seated himself behind his desk,
picked up a pencil and pad, and asked how he could
assist Adam.

Adam had been thinking over the facts all the way
down in the taxi, wondering what the best way was
to proceed. In the end, he decided for straightforward honesty, and began, "In September, I hired
a young woman to act as a typist for me. I acquired
her through a cousin who is a surgeon at Sunnybrook Hospital. You see, I'm writing a book on economic theory, and was finding the entire process
bogged down by my inability to find a typist who
could tolerate my ways."

He watched as Sam made careful notes. "Lynn, the
young woman I hired, was recuperating from a very
serious accident. At the time she started work, her jaw
was still wired up, her face was still somewhat bruised
from plastic surgery to her nose, and one leg was in
a cast."

Adam watched him take all that in, and read from
his expression that he wondered how such a person

could be any use to him. "You are wondering why I would hire someone in this condition."

When Sam nodded, Adam continued, "My cousin, Dr. Tom Dunlop, had discovered that she was an absolute whiz on his laptop computer. In fact, I gather that anyone who had anything to do with Lynn was impressed in one way or another. He also knew from the police report about her that she had worked for the Economic Council in Ottawa, although it was understood that she had just quit her job and was hoping to get a new job in Toronto. Tom knew that I needed an assistant and so he arranged an interview.

"When I first met Lynn in the hospital, I thought Tom was crazy. At that point, her nose was still bandaged, and the remainder of her face was still bruised, but she showed spirit, and when I gave her passages to enter on my laptop computer, she produced work that was flawless. And so I hired her on the spot.

"I'm staying in the home of friends while they travel, and since there was a self-contained suite downstairs, it was arranged that Lynn would get her room and board and a small salary.

"In a very short period of time, I discovered she could handle everything I gave her with ease, and even showed initiative in learning about the subject on her own time. Soon, she was doing far more than just typing, so I gave her a raise in pay and began to train her as a research assistant.

"However, there were other things that were intriguing about her. She spent every spare moment going through my economic books. Her attack on it was not at random. She seemed to have an instinct where to begin, and how to build up her experience. Now she will actually argue with me about economic theory that she has no business understanding.''

By now, Sam had stopped making notes, and was just listening, obviously fascinated. Adam thought for a moment, before beginning the harder part of the narrative. ''At Thanksgiving, my cousin invited the two of us over for dinner. A slip in the conversation let drop a fact every one knew but me. That fact was that Lynn had no memory of her life before the bus accident. She only knew her name because the medical staff addressed her by it. She did not even know how she looked until she was shown her driver's license. Even then, the picture on it was of little help in reconstructing her nose.''

''What bus accident was she injured in?'' interjected Sam.

''It was the terrible multiple collision on Highway 401 on the seventeenth of August, before I had returned to Canada to work on my book.'' It suddenly crossed Adam's mind that Sam might wonder why he was providing such a detailed history, so he explained, ''I am telling you all of this story because I want you to understand my motives.''

Unconscious of his actions, Adam got up and walked over to a window in the office. He stood looking out for a minutes. Finally, with a sigh, he looked Sam Bowers in the eye and said, ''There is no easy way to explain this. I fell in love with Lynn. And I know that even if she should have the same feelings for me, she would never admit them until she knows who she really is.

''With that in mind, I decided to play detective. I read over all the accounts of the accident in the various newspapers, but found nothing. Just as I was about to give up, a headline about a missing Queen's University student, Sarah James, caught my eye. The more I read, the more I was convinced that Lynn was Sarah James.''

At the mention of Sarah James, Sam interrupted. ''I remember that case very well. What convinced you that this girl might be Sarah?''

''First, Sarah was described as a brilliant economics student, and I have just explained the uncanny way that Lynn learned economics. Second, it was thought that Sarah met with some type of foul play. When Lynn came out of the coma she was in after the accident, she had terrifying dreams of confinement in a dark, airless place, and of being chased in some kind of forested area at night. Also, she had fresh scars on her wrists and ankles. These injuries had been noted by the medical staff at Sunnybrook but were viewed as insignificant compared to the very serious injuries caused by the accident, and consequently were ignored.''

''Fascinating and more fascinating,'' said Sam. ''But what do you want me to do?''

Adam was ready for this question and set out his requirements. ''I would like you to find out everything that you can about a stepbrother who showed little interest in the young woman. His name is Dane Copeland. I looked it up and he is president of Copeland-James Associates. I would particularly like to know where he was at the time of her disappearance.''

If Adam had been looking at Sam's face at that precise moment, he would have been surprised at the look of interest that crossed his face when the name Dane Copeland was mentioned. Adam continued. ''I would like to know who benefited from the death of Sarah James.

''Third, I would like you to keep an eye on this Copeland character, and if there should ever seem to be any danger to Lynn, then I would like you to provide unobtrusive protection for her. You may, of course, suggest some other things that should be done.''

Sam Bower studied Adam for a few minutes, and Adam knew that if he had not convinced him, he would not help. Finally, Sam asked, ''What does Lynn say about all of this?''

Sam could see that Adam looked uncomfortable at this question. ''Until I have something definite to present to her, I do not want her to know about this. She is just gaining the confidence to go out and socialize again. In fact, I plan to take her to the Sick Kids' Charity at The Winter Garden next Saturday. My cousin, although not a psychiatrist, feels that it is important that Lynn remember rather than be told of her past. That is why I have started taking her out about town. I'm hoping that she will see or hear something that will jar her memory. In fact, I know very well that something she saw in the Art Gallery of Ontario yesterday seemed familiar. However, she has this notion that she might have been involved in something criminal, and that she could endanger those around her, so she keeps any ideas to herself.''

Adam looked at the detective who was making notes on his pad. Finally, Sam looked up and said, ''Yes, I will do what you request. There are a number of other things I can discover, copies of police reports, etcetera. Right away, I can tell you that the police and I have been very interested in the machinations of Dane Copeland. It is very possible that he will be at your charity since his mother is a patron so I suggest you try to get a ticket for me. I would like to keep an eye on him just in case he recognizes Lynn. For that matter, Lynn might recognize him.''

Suddenly, Adam realized that he had not stressed how different Lynn's face was, so he hastened to explain that it was very possible that she was quite unlike her former self.

Sam considered this information for a moment, and then went on, ''Whether she is recognizable or not, I would also like you to convince Lynn to take a security beeper wherever she goes, to the store, or to the theater. I'll give you one of our latest. It can be worn in a pocket, in a purse or on one's clothing. If she is in danger, all she has to do is pull the pin out, and the sound will disable the assailant. Finally, I will lend you a very high-caliber Polaroid camera. I want you to try to get as many pictures of Lynn as possible, and get them to me so that I can have them copied for my staff.''

The two men continued to discuss strategies for a few more minutes and agreed on the cost of Sam's services. Adam left, feeling much better about his actions and Lynn's safety.

Lynn was mystified. The single-minded writer she had worked for was disappearing before her eyes. Whereas last week he would not have tolerated an interruption, this week he was out more than he was in.

Monday morning he had surprised her by saying that he had had a call from an old high school friend who was in Toronto for a few weeks and that they had decided to meet for breakfast. Adam had rushed out the door after thrusting a list of facts in her hand for her to organize before he returned. Well, she thought, with some annoyance, it was his book. If he wanted to get behind schedule, then that was his privilege. It was ridiculous for her to be irritated.

She worked for an hour but found it hard to concentrate. Finally, in despair, she threw her papers down and took a walk over to her room. For several days now she had had a feeling of unease, as if something was going to happen. She was not sure exactly why she felt uneasy. Maybe it was the change in Adam. He seemed so frightfully preoccupied by something other than the book. At the same time, there were the messages from Adam that had nothing to do with work. She could no longer ignore the fact that he was making it very evident that he was attracted to her. That certainly was confusing because she had no idea how to deal with Adam or the feelings that he stirred in her.

There was something else, something that she had simply refused to recognize at first. She was having tiny bursts of memory. Nothing tangible. Sometimes just a feeling. For example, when she had been in the Henry Moore room at the Art Gallery, she had known for sure that she had been there before. And there had been other things. Occasionally, when Adam and she were working at a particularly difficult concept he wanted incorporated in the book, she would have a flash of information or insight she knew she had not read in any of Adam's texts. Always, these instances lasted for such a short time that she was never able to catch their context.

She was uneasy on another count. She was angry with herself because she had let Adam softsoap her into going to the hospital benefit. Much as she wanted to see the play, she did not want to go to a dance, and Adam had mentioned that there would be dancing after the dinner. She was not even sure that she knew how to dance. Nor was she sure that she could stand a dose of being that close to Adam. She seemed to lose her wits when she was in his arms. And what was she going to wear?

She glanced at her watch. It was only ten o'clock. Taking a chance, she telephoned Allison to see if she was free to go shopping. She needed to buy a gown suitable for the benefit, and the only place she could afford to shop was in the second-hand clothing stores. However, she still did not feel a hundred percent sure of her fashion sense, and also wanted company. She was cheered when Allison agreed with alacrity. In half an hour, Lynn was in a taxi on her way to collect her.

When they reached the stores, Allison turned to Lynn and smiled shyly, "If you must know, I was just about to suffer terminal housewife burnout. I am so glad you called me. I hope that we will have time to go for lunch after."

Together they had blitzed the two stores they knew. In the first one, Allison bought designer jeans and a lovely silk shirt, but Lynn could find nothing. In the second shop, when Lynn described what she needed, the owner said, "I have just the thing for you. It has to be an original for this affair. Also, it must be one from our store in Montreal so that no one recognizes their dress.

"I have just the gown for you," she continued. "It came in yesterday." She went to the clothes rack and took off the most unprepossessing pile of fabric. It hung from the hanger in a sorry fashion, and the only thing that Lynn could find acceptable about it was its color. All shades of blue—delphinium, periwinkle, sky-blue to the palest blue-white. The saleswoman caught Lynn's expression. "Wait unto you try this on before you dismiss it. This gown was worn in Montreal by a ballerina who attended a gala performance at the Place D'Arts. It was a very classy affair; however, I doubt that any of the Toronto crowd was there. This gown was made for your slight figure and your wonderful coloring. Go ahead and try it on."

Allison hurried Lynn into the changing room and assisted her with the dress. It was made of some kind of very fine silk knit. When she held it up, she saw that glass beads were clustered together where the swirls of color were most intense. The dress fit like the proverbial glove. It had a high neck that was done up at the back with tiny bejeweled buttons to give almost a Victorian effect. It had long, tight sleeves that ended in a point at her wrist. However, that was where the period resemblance ended. The back was almost completely bare. The material was only caught up at the neck and waist with the buttons. The fabric fit Lynn as it would a dancer, stressing her slight breasts and slender frame. The skirt was a whirl of blues that clung to her legs as she walked.

When she stepped out of the dressing room and

stood before the mirror, they were all stunned. It was hard to imagine a more suitable gown for the girl staring at Lynn from the mirror. She spun around, and the material bloomed out in a graceful flair.

The owner, ever ready for a sale, produced blue kid shoes that had come with the dress, and luckily, they fit Lynn's feet. It was obvious that they had only been worn once. The final touch was found by Allison who had been poking around the clothes racks. It was a flowing black velvet evening cape. Lynn purchased it with the unhappy thought that she had absolutely nothing left in her bank account and only enough for their lunches in her purse.

Later in the day, Lynn was even more convinced that Adam was up to something when he insisted in taking all kinds of pictures of her with a Polaroid camera she had never seen before. The pictures were for his parents, he said, but when he had no pictures taken of himself, she grew suspicious. Belatedly, he had had her take pictures of him.

He also produced another gadget, a beeper, that he insisted she take with her whenever she left the house. The reason he gave for this was that a young woman had recently been attacked a few streets away.

That evening, after they had put in four hours of very intense work, Adam surprised her by producing two hand-knit stockings of mammoth size. Somewhat embarrassed, he suggested that she might like to fill his stocking Christmas Eve and that he would do hers. Again, Lynn had the feeling that Adam was weaving such a web of belonging around her that she wondered if she would ever survive after the book was finished and they went their separate ways.

*   *   *

In the end, Adam was unable to see Alain until Friday because Alain was tied up with end-of-term exams. When Adam had talked to Alain, he had stressed that the subject he wished to discuss had nothing to do with economics. In fact, he had stressed that he wanted Alain to help him with a personal problem, and that he would prefer it if Alain mentioned their meeting to no one. If Alain was mystified, he was too well-mannered to say so. Adam had asked him to choose a quiet restaurant with excellent cuisine as lunch would be his treat.

Since the weather had turned warm, the driving conditions were excellent and Adam timed the three-hour trip to Kingston perfectly. He arrived in the old section of the lime-stoned city that sat at the eastern end of Lake Ontario just as the noon-hour bells rang from the nearby cathedral. Alain was already in the restaurant when Adam came in, and they were given a table upstairs that allowed them to look out over the street below. They talked about generalities until their order was given. Then Adam could contain his curiosity no longer. Taking a sip of wine, he watched the young man opposite him as he tried to choose the right words.

Finally, he began. "The reason I asked you to meet me is that I think that you can provide me with some information I need for a very private purpose. I assure you that my use of this information is all legal and above board." Adam took another sip of wine, and then continued. "I am hoping that you might be able to tell me about Sarah James, the student who did not come to her interview with me as planned and who, I understand, died last autumn.''

Alain did not try to hide his surprise. Adam Stone wanted to know about Sarah? Why? he wondered. Finally gathering his wits, he asked, "What would you like to know about Sarah?"

"Everything," Adam replied. "What she looked like, her personality, the quality of her studies. Just everything."

Alain thought for a few minutes. Finally, he said, "It's not easy for me to talk about Sarah. I was extremely fond of her."

Alain was surprised when the color left Adam's face, as he asked sharply, "You were romantically involved with her?"

Alain hastened to dissuade him of the idea. "Heavens, no. I am engaged to a doctor who has been working on her internship in Quebec City these last two years." Alain could almost see Adam slump with relief. He continued, "Sarah was one of seven of us in the master's program last year. I have been told by my professors that we were an exceptional lot. I know that we were all bright, but by far the brightest of the class was Sarah."

The waiter came with their first course, a soup. When he left, Alain went on. "What was also exceptional about the group was that we all got on very well. There were three girls and four fellows in the class. We did everything together—both studying and socializing. For Sarah, it seemed to have been the first time that she had ever been part of a group, and she blossomed before our eyes."

Adam interrupted. "Why do you think that?"

Alain chose his words carefully, "Sarah had a facial deformity that must have caused her grief, socially, for years. We prepared several seminars together, and I got to know her rather well. She told me that as the condition worsened through adolescence, she was more and more ostracized by the girls in the private school she attended. She did her undergraduate work at the University of Toronto, and I think she was just as lonely there. She stayed in residence but I gather she made no real friends. And the undergraduate classes are always so large that she was just lost in the crowds."

At Alain's words, Adam felt a surge of excitement. More proof that Lynn was Sarah, for hadn't Tom described just such a deformity. "Describe the facial deformity to me," demanded Adam.

"Sarah had a congenital condition of the jaw, and as she entered adolescence, the jaw began to drop down and back. It interfered with her speech and her ability to eat."

"But why wasn't it fixed? Surely, if her parents could send her to a private school and university, they could afford to have it corrected."

"Well, that was another unfortunate thing about Sarah. Her parents had split up before she was even born. She lived with her mother just outside of town here until she was eleven when her mother died of cancer. At that point, she was sent to her father in Toronto who had remarried, and it seems could not bear the sight of her. Her stepmother and her stepbrother were equally unpleasant to her. It seems that she was never made welcome in her father's home. In fact, during the school year she was boarded even though her father's house was only a bus-ride away, and in the summers she was sent to camp.''

The waiter interrupted them with the main course, and Adam waited impatiently until Alain could continue his story. After they had eaten for a few minutes, Adam urged Alain on by saying, ''You have still not explained why her jaw was not repaired.''

''Well, according to Sarah, while her father was alive there was no regular procedure done to cure the malady. Also, it was felt that any effort to correct it had to be done after Sarah had finished growing. By the time Sarah was old enough for the surgery, if it existed, there was no money. Her father, a prominent Toronto investor and millionaire to boot, died and left only enough money to educate her until she finished her undergraduate degree. He left his fortune to the wife and stepson.''

By now Adam was sure he was hearing the story of Lynn's life, and it was all he could do to remain unmoved by the facts Alain was giving him. Alain continued. ''Sarah actually paid for her own schooling last year by earning good scholarships and by being a don in the residence. And this year, she earned the top scholarship given at Queen's as well as a teaching position. When she disappeared, the position and the scholarship were given to me. It is one of my greatest regrets that I should profit from her tragedy.''

They both sat quietly for a few minutes. Finally, Adam said, ''You really have not told me anything about Sarah's appearance except that she had a deformed jaw. Could you fill me in with more detail?''

''Sarah was about five feet, four inches. She was

not stout, just a little heavy. I think that she ate a lot to make up for everything else. She had the most beautiful long black hair. It hung almost to her waist. And her eyes were an incredible blue. They used to remind me of a bouquet of irises in the sunshine. She had a . . . '' Alain stopped suddenly, and a faraway look came over his face. And then, he looked directly at Adam. ''Your assistant, Lynn, reminds me of her.'' And when Adam made no answer, he continued, ''And you think that Lynn is Sarah? Right? But how could that be?''

Adam nodded, and then said, ''That's what I am attempting to figure out.'' And then he told him every detail: Lynn's accident, her loss of memory, her nightmares, and the scars. ''The fact that you made the connection just confirms my theory. However, there are still many unanswered questions, and I think that there is someone who would do her harm if it ever became known that she was still alive. I trust that I can depend on your complete confidence in this matter.''

Alain assured him that he could. But he still appeared puzzled. ''I'm afraid that I'm still very confused. When was this accident Sarah . . . er . . . Lynn was in?''

Adam told him the date, and Alain exclaimed, ''That's strange. Sarah left Kingston the day before that. She was going to Toronto for two purposes. Her stepbrother had allowed her to stay in a bachelor apartment above the garage in her father's Toronto home until she finished her education. She intended to remove the few belongings that she had from the apartment and take them to Kingston. Because of her scholarship and teaching job, she was now able to afford her own small apartment. She was terribly excited about this.''

''And the other reason?'' Adam asked.

''Strangely enough, she had an appointment to see a maxillofacial surgeon about the correction of her jaw. Sarah half-hoped that she could have the surgery done before the school year began; however, she had no idea just how long recovery from the operation would take.''

Adam considered this information, then continued, ''There is something else I need. Is there any possibility that you would have a picture of Sarah? And would you be able to take me out to where she lived with her mother?''

''Yes, I have a few very poor shots of Sarah, and I would be happy to lend them to you. I also have the time to take you out to where Sarah lived.''

But as Adam called for the waiter for his check, Alain went on to say, ''Adam, I do not think I have given you a complete picture of Sarah yet. In spite of the fact that Sarah was somewhat disfigured by her jaw, and had lived quite a lonely life until she got to Queen's, she was also one of the most completely balanced personalities I know. She was well-loved in her mother's home, and, as she explained to me, given such a good sense of her self-worth that it did not matter how her father had treated her, or that she had the problem with the jaw. She knew that she was good at her studies, and she also knew that she was going to have her face repaired. She did not expect to be beautiful when it was corrected as she still would have her father's arrogant nose, but she explained to me that it would give her style and individuality, and that she was quite prepared to live happily with her face if she could just speak clearly and eat with ease.''

After Adam had settled the bill, they drove in Adam's car to Alain's apartment. Adam went up with Alain and waited while he searched for the photographs. When he found them, he apologized. ''There are only three that include Sarah. She really hated having her picture taken. She even refused to have her graduation picture taken. As you can see, these are not much. The police were never able to use them in the newspapers.''

Adam studied the three shots. In the first, he saw the figure of a young woman in jeans taken from the back. Her hair was long, but the light caught it, and Adam had no doubt that it was Lynn's. The fact that she weighed a little more was also evident. Almost apologetically, Alain pointed out, ''Sarah didn't spend much on clothes. I rarely recall her in anything but jeans and a shirt.''

In the second picture, Sarah was caught in profile, but the picture was small, as she was one of a laughing group of students holding up pieces of pizza in the air. ''We were celebrating the end of exams,'' Alain explained.

The last picture was a closeup, taken over the head of another student. There, looking at him, was his Lynn. Those were her eyes and eyebrows. Her hair had been pulled back from her forehead and held by some kind of clip. Alain touched the photograph almost reverently. ''I sneaked this picture with a closeup lens. It was just my luck that the guy in front of her stood just as I fired the shutter. I was never able to get another.''

Alain looked at Adam for a minute, and then shook his head. ''You know, it is just sinking in that Sarah is alive, and I have actually seen her. Now that I think about it, I can hardly believe that I did not recognize her at your place. Then Alain asked, ''What did Sarah say when you told her what you suspected?''

''Now you come to a major problem,'' replied Adam. ''I have not told Lynn about any of this. My cousin was the surgeon who rebuilt her jaw, and he felt, after discussing such a hypothetical case with a psychiatrist colleague, that it would be best if Lynn could recall the events naturally. Consequently I have been taking Lynn out around Toronto sightseeing and going to parties, in the hope that something will ring a bell.

''You realize,'' Adam went on, ''there is a risk in all of this. I think that there is no doubt that someone tried to do away with Lynn, and presently thinks that he has succeeded. Certainly, her new face is a good disguise, but her voice and manner might still be recognizable. That is why I employed a detective agency to assist. Now that I am sure, I will ask them to keep an eye on her at all times. I am also having them check out her stepbrother.''

While Adam had been telling Alain this, he was aware that the young man was mulling something over. Finally, Alain spit it out. ''Would you mind telling me why you are going to such expense and effort over this?''

''I am sure you may suspect already,'' grinned Adam. ''For the record, I love her deeply, and I know that even if she were to love me, she would never admit it while she cannot remember.''

Adam stood up. ''Come on, now. Take me out to her mother's place and then I have to get back to Toronto.''

The property on which Sarah's mother's house was located ran from the highway right down to the St. Lawrence River. Alain described her home as they drove out of town. ''The house is a very old limestone farmhouse. Such buildings are worth a fortune nowadays. Half the yuppies in the area have bought them and fixed them up. I know that Sarah dreamed of the day when she could afford to live in hers.''

''You mean the house belongs to Lynn?'' asked Adam.

''Yes, it does. However, Sarah's mother's estate was managed by the father, and then by the stepbrother until her twenty-third birthday when she would gain control over the house and land. Sarah's twenty-third birthday would have been in November. She used to drive out here and walk around the house. It broke her heart that it was all boarded up. I could never think why the stepbrother did not just hand it over when she came to Kingston. Sarah was certainly capable of handling her own affairs.''

''I gather that Lynn's mother was not well off. How did she manage to make a living?''

''Now, that's interesting,'' replied Alain. ''The house and land were the only settlement that Sarah's mother received when she was divorced. Sarah's mother, however, was an artist and managed to make a living at her craft. Her paintings are considered very valuable now. Unfortunately, Sarah only had one and she would never sell it.''

A thrill of excitement curled up Adam's spine. ''That's the last piece of the puzzle, Alain. Because I am sure I know her mother's name—Martine Hébért. Right?''

''Now, how did you know that?

''Because Lynn has been fascinated by one of her paintings that the Brownings, who own the house I am renting, have hanging in the suite that Lynn uses.''

By then, they had reached the property, and Alain directed Adam up a lane that led to the house. ''That's strange,'' he exclaimed as they got closer. A tall temporary fence encircled the house, and a large sign proclaimed: YOU ARE VIEWING THE LOCATION OF THE NEW ST. LAWRENCE HEIGHTS. DUE TO BEGIN CONSTRUCTION NEXT MAY. DOWN-PAYMENT NOW WILL ENSURE WATERFRONT PROPERTY.

''Something's really fishy here, Adam. Who would be able to build on this property? Lynn told me she had the deed in a safe place. She also told me that she left a will in the same safe place so that if anything happened to her, her creep of a stepbrother could not get his hands on it. To my knowledge, neither the will nor the deed have been found.''

Already, Adam was making a note of the name of the company that claimed to be building the project. ''Seaway Properties. Now whose company would that be, I wonder? I'll telephone this information to Sam Bowers, my investigator, before I start home. He should have the answer by the time I reach Toronto.''

Adam said good-bye to Alain after getting his parents' address and telephone number where he would be from the next day until the new term began. He promised that he would let him know how the investigation proceeded. Before leaving Kingston, Adam had a long telephone conversation with Sam Bowers.

Lynn sighed and put the last supper dish away in the cupboard. She felt at loose ends. Adam had left a mountain of work to be done when he had hurried out that morning saying that he would be gone all day, but she had managed to finish it before she stopped for supper, leaving far too much time for her to think.

Things were shifting and changing so fast. *She* was changing. It had been so easy when she had first come there. All her energies had been focused on discovering her skills and in finding out about herself. But now, she felt more secure, and her wayward mind spent far too much time thinking about Adam and her reactions to him. When they were working on ideas, they seemed so in tune that they could almost read each other's minds. However, all the rest of the time she was conscious that her attention was on Adam, watching him, admiring him, wanting to touch him. She was sure this must have been how it was when she was an adolescent; however, it seemed more than a teenage reaction. She felt such joy when she was with him. And yet, she could not help but wonder if she had had the same experience in her former existence. It was all very confusing. Wearily, she went into her room and turned on the radio to listen to the CBC news. After a minute, she realized she had tuned into an item on violence against women. For some reason, she could not stomach the topic, and was in the act of pushing the button to change the station when the name Sarah James was mentioned. She stopped and listened. She was sure that was the name of the girl who had now shown up for the interview with Adam.

She caught only a very short portion of the program. The commentator was summarizing the last known actions of the girl, and then a police detective asked the public to come forward with any information they thought would assist them to locate the girl or her body. A wave of nausea swept over Lynn at the thought of the poor girl's body in some ditch.

The program left her even more restless. She wandered around the house and finally settled in the solarium before the twinkling Christmas tree. There were presents under it now. Some were for the Dunlops while others appeared mysteriously with her name on them. Adam was certainly having fun getting ready for Christmas, she thought. He had even made it possible for her to participate. The evening after she had blown the bundle on her dress so to speak, Adam had insisted on giving her a Christmas bonus. It was a ridiculous sum, and she was ready to argue, but the look in Adam's eye had stopped her. Consequently she had been able to purchase articles for his stocking which she hid in her closet, and a number of presents, both serious and silly. Every few days, she put another gift under the tree. It amused her when Adam came into the room each evening and surreptitiously checked the parcels. Another benefit of the Christmas gift exchange was that she had gained sufficient courage to go out shopping on her own.

Unable to curb her restlessness, Lynn returned to work in the solarium and was still at the computer when Adam came in. He seemed preoccupied, and spent only a short time with her before turning in. The only information he gave her about his day was to say that he had seen his friend, Sam Bowers, and that Sam would be attending the theater with them the next night.

Sam Bowers thought, as he watched Adam Stone make him a drink, that the economist suited the sophisticated surroundings of the Brownings' living room. He had done his homework on this man and learned that he was a brilliant, creative thinker. Yet none of this exclusive ability set him off as odd or eccentric. Instead, he seemed a highly polished animal, moving with easy grace as he completed his task.

Sam was uneasy about this evening's outing. There were too many unanswered questions about this case. His initial instinct had been to suggest that Adam cancel, no matter how beneficial the cause, and now he wished he had.

Ever since Adam's interview, he and his team had been working flat out. He had pulled all the strings he could to get information from the Fraud Squad about Sarah's stepbrother.

Dane Copeland, it seemed, had taken the company of Copeland-James into very deep water since the death of Cyril James. Too often, it was felt, he had taken the funds of his investors and used them for various developmental schemes, yet no one had been able to catch him. He was as wily as a fox, and always seemed to be two steps ahead of the law. That is, until now. In the case of the St. Lawrence Heights Development, the police thought that they might finally have a chance of catching him.

The disappearance of his stepsister had put a hold on this development when it became clear that Copeland had been gathering the funds of investors to develop land for which he did not have the deed. In fact, no one had the deed. What seemed to be saving Copeland from arrest at that moment was the fine print in Cyril James's will where it stated that Copeland was to continue to administer the small amount of capital left by his ex-wife, Sarah's mother, for the benefit of Sarah. Copeland argued that in selling the home and land that had belonged to Sarah, he had hoped to make Sarah a fortune. The police found this theory hard to swallow now that the girl had disappeared and there was neither a deed for the land, nor the girl's will.

The Fraud Squad captain claimed that there had been a large reorganization of funds between August seventeenth and the time when it was discovered that Sarah had disappeared. The police felt that Copeland had known she had disappeared, but he had switched the funds so cleverly that, so far, they had not been able to make a direct link between the switch and her disappearance. The fact that there was almost a three-week interval before she was found missing, and then another long period of time before the car was found, made it impossible to pin down Copeland. His claim that he had been on a fishing holiday up in the lakes northwest of Kingston and Ottawa had been verified. On the other hand, he was near enough to Toronto to have been able to come in for a day or night unnoticed and the lakes were sufficiently isolated that it was easy for Copeland to claim he had been there all the time.

Sam was also curious about the identity of the body on the bus. Why had everyone been so sure that Lynn was actually Lynn MacDougall? That was something he had forgotten to ask Adam.

So tonight, if they could manage it, or at the latest, tomorrow, he wanted another conference with Adam. He was just about to make this request as Adam handed him his drink when a door opened off the end of the living room and a young woman entered.

Sam's drink never made it to his lips. Instead, he stood transfixed. No wonder Adam Stone was so keen on solving the mystery! Standing before him, looking out of incredible eyes that were so clearly those in the photographs Adam had given him, was a lovely young woman clad in a gown of swirling blues that emphasized her slight figure and heightened the color of her eyes. She approached shyly, her self-consciousness so obviously at odds with her appearance that Sam was intrigued.

Sam was not the only one affected. For a moment, Adam stood like one in a dream, and then he moved forward, took her hand and said, "How lovely you look tonight, Lynn. Come and meet my friend, Sam Bowers."

She turned and smiled at Sam, took his hand and welcomed him. He was taken by the intelligent way her eyes examined him, and thought that Adam had better be very careful how he proceeded.

For the next few minutes, as they sipped their drinks

and exchanged small talk, Sam amused himself by watching the two of them together. Whether she knew it or not, Lynn seemed to be as aware of Adam as he was of her, and his heart turned over with pain and regret. How they reminded him of himself and his wife, Connie, when they had fallen in love. Well, he promised himself, he could do nothing about the loss of his wife, but he could do his best to protect this young woman, to help Adam solve the mystery of her identity and to discover the name of her enemy. With this resolution, his unease about the evening's events lessened somewhat. As they got their coats and headed out for the waiting limousine, Sam was quietly able to arrange for a conference at the house the next morning at nine.

Lynn sat, bemused, in the luxurious gray limousine with which Adam had surprised her. As he had helped her into it, he had murmured, "Your coach, mademoiselle."

I wonder if he really does realize that all this feels like a fairy tale, she thought. Nothing seems real. Not my beautiful dress, this elegant cape or the two handsome men sitting with me.

While she had been getting dressed, excitement had sustained her, but now, reality was taking over. Tonight she was going to a crowded theater, and she felt uneasy about it. She had not slept well the previous night. Her rest had been haunted by dreams, old ones, and new ones about that poor girl she had heard about on the news special. Nervously, she rubbed her wrists under the protective covering of her dress's long sleeves. Adam noticed the action, reached over and took one cold hand and held it. She shouldn't be frightened, she thought, Adam was with her, and by now, she knew that he would do everything in his power to keep her safe. Why then did she have this feeling, this premonition, that things weren't right?

And Sam Bowers. There was definitely something strange about him. Somehow, the two men's conversation did not quite ring true. Adam had said they were old friends, but they did not seem relaxed enough for this.

Sam asked Adam if he had ever been in the Elgin or the Winter Garden theaters. When Adam answered that he had not, Sam began to describe them. They had been a part of the famous chain of Loew's vaudeville theaters built in 1913 and 1914. Sam smiled at Lynn and said, "Marcus Loew was a wily entrepreneur. Yonge Street property was expensive so instead of placing the theater on the street, he purchased only enough land to accommodate the box office and entrance. Cleverly, he created a long lobby that took the patrons to the main body of the theater located on the less expensive property on the street behind. Then, to get the most out of that space, he built one theater on top of the other."

This caught Adam's interest and the conversation between the two men flowed back and forth. Sitting close to Adam, holding his hand firmly, she concentrated on gathering her courage and overcoming her nervousness. Surely her finery would disguise her. She knew that she hardly recognized herself in her lovely gown. Adam must have sensed her disquiet because he leaned over and whispered, "Quit worrying. No one recognized Cinderella at the ball and no one will recognize you.''

She smiled quietly to herself at the reference and then switched her attention back to the men's conversation. The Ontario Heritage Foundation had restored the theaters, and the downstairs theater, now named the Elgin, had opened with a fine production of the show *CATS*. However, they were going to the upstairs theater, The Winter Garden. Sam smiled at her and said, ''I don't think I will tell you anything about it so that you will be surprised.''

At that moment, the limousine pulled to a stop in front of the theaters. Glancing out the window, Lynn was appalled to see that the sidewalk before the entrance was completely jammed with people either waiting for others, or making their way into the theater. Anxiety spread through her and she was aware of the pumping of her heart. Adam turned to her, and noting her pallor, hastened to assure her. ''Come on, Cinderella. Sam and I will be your Prince Charmings. We'll each take an arm and clear the way through this crowd in a minute.'' Gallantly, the two men exited the car and held the door open as she got out. Immediately, they each extended an arm for her to take, and headed into the crowd.

Once they had passed by the box office that sat in the center of the entrance and passed through the lobby doors, the crowd spread out, and they were able to stop and admire the newly refurbished lobby. It was a place of dulled gold and black. Marbelized columns set off gilt-trimmed mirrors and elegant damask-covered walls. Christmas trees, decorated in gold and covered with myriads of tiny white lights, stood tall before each set of mirrors. As they moved along, Lynn could see the three of them in the mirrors. Their images were muted in the subdued light, and she had the same feeling she had had so many times before, that of playing a role, of being someone other than herself, for the slender creature in the long black cloak with the large eyes and pale complexion seemed far removed from her.

When they had passed through the lobby to the body of the theater, Adam led them away from the great staircase that the crowd was moving up and took them to ornate elevator doors, insisting that they should save Lynn's leg for dancing. They were early enough that when they exited from the elevator they could walk about the handsome promenades of The Winter Garden. Tall Christmas trees stood proudly in these lobbies. A choir sang Christmas carols as the patrons walked around admiring two immense canvas backdrops that had been saved from vaudeville times. "When an artist came to perform," Sam explained, "he or she could ask for any one of approximately one hundred and fifty backdrops available."

A buzzer sounded and the patrons, who like themselves had been admiring the restored scenery, moved on into the theater. To say that Lynn was surprised with her first view of the theater was to put it mildly. She felt as if she had wandered into a strange exotic world where overhead, thousands of russet beech leaves hung suspended from the ceiling of the theater and the balcony. Nestled in among the leaves were tiny four-sided colored glass lanterns. On whitewashed walls, delicate hand-painted rosebushes with pink blooms spread up trellises toward the trembling beech leaves. She turned to the men in amazement and Sam grinned with delight at her wonder. "I knew that it would spoil it for you if I described it ahead of time."

"It's a true winter garden," she said in wonder, and reached up and tried to touch the leaves.

"They are real," laughed Sam at her attempt. "Volunteers helped collect the leaves and prepare them so that they could be hung."

So enthralled was Lynn with the theater that she forgot her nervousness and settled into the plush green velvet seat ready to enjoy the show. Within minutes, she was lost in the story and music. At a particularly touching incident onstage, she turned and smiled at Adam, and he reached out, took her hand, and held it for the rest of the act. She sat there in a sort of euphoria. The warmth and steadiness of his grip seemed to sharpen every sense so that each word of dialogue, each actor's gesture, each note of music seemed intensified and more beautiful. And Sam, noting their hands, vowed again that nothing was going to come between these lovers.

When the lights came on at intermission, Lynn was still under the spell of the play as she followed Adam out into the aisle of the theater. Bending slightly to pick up the folds of her dress, she moved into the aisle only to collide against a man who was looking behind him as he proceeded out. Sam watched the collision but was too far away to stop it from happening. He saw Lynn stumble, saw the man turn and steady her with his hand, and then saw him almost yank her toward him and exclaim, "You!"

Even as he realized with horror the identity of the man, he heard Lynn say, "You know me?"

That seemed to startle the man and he dropped her arm and replied in a rather confused and embarrassed manner, "Umm, actually, no, I don't. But you look very much like a woman in a painting I have in my collection at home."

By this time, Adam had realized that something had happened and returned to Lynn while Sam gained a spot beside her. The man smiled suavely at them both, apologized again for being so clumsy, and hurried up the aisle to the side of an older woman.

Made uneasy by the incident, Lynn took Adam's arm and held tightly until they reached the lobby where the well-heeled crowd was sipping drinks and nibbling hors d'oeuvres. Only then was Sam able to whisper to Adam that the man who had bumped into Lynn was none other than Dane Copeland. He excused himself, found a telephone, and arranged for a tail to be put on Copeland around the clock just in case he had recognized Lynn.

When the show was over, the audience gathered in one of the elegant lobbies for a most splendid buffet dinner. Long tables of food were decorated with colorful Christmas flowers, and one was crowned with the pièce de résistance, a brilliant ice-carving of Santa Claus landing on the hospital rooftop. Restigouche salmon in aspic and rare roast beef were surrounded by delicately prepared vegetables and salads. A separate table was loaded with desserts guaranteed to satisfy any sweet tooth.

After the three of them had settled at the table of their hostess, Adam suggested that he bring a plate of food for Lynn as well as himself, however, Lynn refused this. She wanted to walk along the table and admire its splendors, and accompanied both Adam and Sam to the buffet. It was while she was selecting her food that she noticed the man who had bumped into her. He was sitting at a nearby table with the older woman she had seen just ahead of him in the theater aisle. The woman was no doubt his mother, she thought, as she had the same deep-set eyes and determined jaw. Lynn shivered when she remembered those eyes—as cold and gray as Adam's were warm. And they watched her now under hooded lids.

Nervously, she turned to the buffet to fill her plate, but her pleasure in the feast before her was gone. Unbidden came a memory of the man's solid frame and the hard hands that had steadied her, and a shaft of dread pierced her. She watched him surreptitiously as she walked back to her seat with her plateful of food. His eyes still followed her. Does he know me? Could he be the one who was after me or is it that he is trying to decide if I really do look like someone in his picture? If that is true, she thought with growing excitement, possibly the picture is a clue to my identity.

While they were finishing their dessert, she became aware that the man was approaching the table. She felt Adam tense and wondered why.

The man stopped to greet their hostess, and then turned to Lynn and said smoothly, "Please let me introduce myself. My name is Dane Copeland." And he held his hand out in a gesture that demanded that she take it and introduce herself. He continued, "You really do have an amazing resemblance to a woman in

a picture in my collection, only you are younger.''
Lynn was aware that as he spoke he studied her carefully. He went on, ''I am sorry that I startled you.''
And with a very charming smile and a few words to
another man at the table, he returned to his seat. But
Lynn was uneasy. That trip to the table had been de-
liberate, and the onceover he had given her had been
thorough.

At that point speeches were given thanking everyone for making the evening such a success and an-
nouncing the amount raised. Then the music began,
and before Lynn had a chance to get nervous, Adam
took her hand and pulled her toward the dance floor.

When Adam turned to her, she went into his arms
hesitantly, not sure just how well she would be able
to dance. At first they moved around politely, hardly
talking. But then the dance floor became more
crowded. Adam pulled her against him, and held her
hand between them. Beneath it, she could feel the
beating of his heart, and was surrounded by the scent
that was Adam; that combination of aftershave and his
own particular male fragrance that urged her to lean
into him. As they moved slowly, Adam caressed her
back and buried his face against her hair.

She was lost, lost in a wash of sensation like none
she could remember experiencing, isolated from
everything else but Adam's hard body against the softness of hers, captured in a moment of time so shattering that she wondered if her legs would hold her.
She knew that she never wanted the dance to end, that
she could cheerfully end her days in the mindless
pleasure of this moment.

Adam must have felt it, too, because when the music ended and the lights came on he seemed almost as dazed as she was, and kept her clasped close to his side as they returned to their table. They were both embarrassed when they remembered Sam had been on his own, but when Adam tried to apologize, Sam smiled and said not to worry, that he had just drummed up some business with one of the other guests.

Clad once more in her black velvet cape, Lynn allowed herself to be handed into the limousine and sat close to Adam, his arm around her as the two men arranged to meet at the house for breakfast the next day. Lynn wondered idly why Adam had not invited his friend to stay the night, then dismissed the thought when they reached home. Adam took her hand and led her up to the door. When he had unlocked the door and turned off the security system, he turned and suggested, "How would you like a drink of some kind before you turn in? We could have it in the solarium and enjoy the lights of the Christmas tree."

She would have done anything he asked of her at this point, she thought. Jump in the pool or tap dance on the kitchen table. I'm crazy, she thought, to let myself float along like this. I know that it isn't right, that I should be trying to solve the problem of my identity, not swooning in his arms, but darn it, I never felt like this before and I may never again. Tonight I am not going to worry. I am just going to enjoy . . . *enjoy what?* a little voice asked. She ignored it, and followed Adam into the kitchen.

Together they prepared their drinks, he a scotch and she a hot chocolate, and then they went into the solarium, turned on the Christmas tree lights, and in their soft glow, sat together on the chesterfield. For a while they discussed the show and the rest of the evening, and then Adam turned to her and gently pulled her over to him. Carefully, he took her face between his hands and studied it in the pale light. As he ran his thumb across her lips, he whispered, ''You are so incredibly lovely,'' and bent down and began a kiss that in its first seconds demolished all her defenses. As his lips stroked and tasted, she melted into his arms, and wound her arms around his neck. As he deepened the kiss, she responded, overcome with a desire to give as much pleasure as she was receiving.

She was unaware that her hands were caressing Adam beneath his jacket, stroking the long, hard muscles of his back. She was unaware of everything but Adam's mouth on her lips, her eyes, her chin, her throat, and Adam's hands on her back, sliding across its smoothness and making circles of sensation. She must have said his name, for suddenly he tensed and then went to end the embrace. When she objected, he hushed her and said, ''It's all right. Let's just hold each other for a while.'' For a long while they lay there, without talking, quietly coming back to earth. Gently he stroked her hair, calming her, and then his hand stopped and she realized that he had drifted off to sleep, her head against his shoulder, his arms still around her.

She lay with him, wondering how it was that only now the truth was so obvious. She loved him. All the reasons she had for not getting close to anyone, for waiting to discover her identity had been delaying tac tics, strategies to keep her from admitting her feelings.

And now, all those reasons seemed irrelevant. She loved Adam. She wanted him, needed him. Nothing in her future would be right without him.

Adam stirred, mumbled her name and then relaxed again. What a coward she had been, hiding behind Adam in this fortress house, living only in the safe circle of the garden and the granite walls. But that would change! Tightening her arms around him, she vowed to discover who she was. She would begin tomorrow. She would start before breakfast by going for a walk down the street that made her so nervous and see if it stirred any memories. Next, she would see if Adam would accompany her to the home of Dane Copeland to see the painting. Maybe there was a clue there. They could also discuss her bilingual ability, something that she had almost forgotten about. Also, she would contact the student from Queen's, Alain. He had thought that she reminded him of someone. Finally, she would check on the newspaper articles about the accident and also ask Tom to get copies of the accident reports that must have been made when they brought her into the hospital.

She shook her head at her blindness. How could she not have known that she loved Adam? How could she have hidden all these obvious courses of action from herself for so long? She could have been solving her mystery weeks ago.

When Adam finally stirred and woke with a start, she had her agenda ready. Giving him a final kiss good-night, she hurried off to bed before it crossed his mind that there was much they needed discuss.

*   *   *

Adam woke with a start. A noise had disturbed him. It sounded like a door closing. He glanced at the clock and was startled to see it was 8:30. Hurriedly, he showered and dressed. He wanted to talk to Lynn before Sam came. After last night, when she had responded to him so openly, he knew that there could be no more secrets. He had to tell her that he had employed Sam, and that he suspected that he knew who she really was.

He also had to decide whether now was the time to tell her how he felt about her. There was so much to consider. As Sarah, she had not finished her education or achieved her career goals. If Lynn was to remember her life as Sarah, would she want to tie herself to a man his age? He wanted that tie. He wanted marriage. He wanted to ensure her presence in all areas of his life and he was ready to modify his career to accommodate her needs. Wryly, he smiled to himself. Was it only a few weeks ago that he had been asserting that he wanted to be free to roam?

Adam was relieved when he came downstairs to see that Lynn's door was open. She was probably in the kitchen. However, when he went in there was no sign of her, or of the usual coffee waiting in the coffeemaker. Only a note stood ominously against an empty coffeemaker. Only a note stood ominously against an empty coffee cup. A whisper of unease shivered down Adam's spine as he picked it up and read: *8:25. Have gone for a walk while the weather is still good. Have the coffee on when I get back! Shouldn't be more than half an hour—Lynn. P.S. I have my beeper with me.*

"I don't like this," he thought uneasily.

* * *

Lynn took a breath of the spring-like air and smiled. What a delight it was to be able to stride along on this balmy morning, one of the shortest in the year, and smell the moist grass. The early sun gilded the leafless trees, and sparrows and chickadees chattered among their branches. A cat wandered across the lawn of one of the mansions that lined the street, stopping to savor interesting odors.

Maybe the morning is some kind of omen, she thought, for there should have been cold winds and snow. In fact, a storm was forecast for later that day. Finally, she reached the entrance to the street. Without the heavily leaved trees it seemed less ominous, brighter, lighter, and yet, as she entered it, she could not ignore the shiver of apprehension that filled her. Why? she wondered.

Well, she thought, there is only one way to find out, and taking a deep breath, she began her descent.

She walked quickly to keep up her courage. It was an older street than the one on which the Brownings lived. Large stone mansions of two and three stories were placed well back on well-kept properties, often guarded by stone walls and pretentious stone entrances. Many were almost hidden by the carefully placed trees and shrubs. The road curved down to the right and finally reached a dead end. Here there was a turnaround in which a car and van were parked. Beyond this there was a barrier, and a path that led into a ravine. Obviously, people drove to the ravine and then walked its trails. Lynn stood looking down into it. In the morning light it was a place of peace and beauty. Sun sought its way down through the pines, cedars and leafless maples and oaks to dapple its paths.

Nothing in it seemed threatening or, for that matter, familiar. Nor had the houses along the street stirred any recollection. And yet, a feeling of unease kept her taut with nervousness.

Still, it had been worth a try. Anything was worth a try. Maybe she would see something that would trigger a memory as she walked back up.

She was rounding the curve when she came nose to nose with a jogger. Surprised, she was aware of the man's voice before she really saw him and then her heart stilled with apprehension. Dane Copeland!

He reacted more quickly than she did. "Ms. MacDougall. I didn't know you lived in my neighborhood."

Startled, she looked into his face and felt the blood freeze in her veins. Those eyes! she thought. Just for a moment, they seemed significant, and then the sensation was gone. She searched his face but could find no familiarity of feature. She was sure that she did not know him.

Taking a step back, Lynn took a big breath and thought, okay, Lynn, this is it. Your life has been full of bizarre coincidences. Make this one work for you. Do it for Adam.

Summoning up her most nonchalant expression, she responded, "Nor I you. But then, this is the first day that I have walked this far. Usually, I stop at the top of the hill. It was so lovely out today that I decided to explore. Do you jog every morning?"

The big man still blocked her way but he responded with the same charm he had used the night before. "I jog all year, weather permitting."

"Well, you are made of sterner stuff than I am. I

prefer to walk in the daylight and in pleasant weather. In fact, we usually walk around noon.'' Now, why did I feel it was necessary to throw in the *we*, she wondered?

Just at that moment another jogger approached them, paused to say hello, and continued down the street toward the ravine. The interruption gave Lynn time to think. Dane Copeland must live nearby. Maybe she could see the picture. He need not know that it was important. She could pretend curiosity. The man before her made her nervous, but the stakes were high. She wanted to know who she was. Only then could she seriously entertain her feelings for Adam.

She turned to the houses and asked, ''Do you live around here?''

''Right here,'' he replied, and pointed to a huge mansion set back behind high stone walls. Through the gates, she could see it was ivy-covered and stood on impressive grounds.

''It's a lovely home. So elegant. So traditional.''

She watched the big man beam at these remarks. ''Oh, by the way,'' she continued, ''I meant to ask you, what is the woman like in the picture, and why do I remind you of her?''

He responded just as she had hoped. ''Would you like to see the painting? Maybe we can figure out some connection between you and the woman.''

It had been too simple, she thought uneasily. However, desperate needs required desperate measures. ''I'd love to see it. I have never known anyone in an oil painting. I was born in Cape Breton and no one there could afford to have their picture painted.'' If there was danger and he did have something to do with her past that should lead him astray.

In a leisurely fashion they walked between two pillars and up the driveway toward the house. At the last minute they veered toward a large attached coach house that appeared to have an apartment above it. Why weren't they going to the house? Alarmed, she slipped her hand into her jacket and positioned her beeper, just in case. "Do you keep your paintings in the coach house? Is it a sort of gallery?"

Cold gray eyes watched her as he replied, "No, but this painting is in an office I keep above the garage, waiting for the manager of the Newland Gallery to pick it up and change the frame. It really does not do much for the painting. I think the artist must have been hard up when the picture was framed."

Lynn was about to ask about the artist when they arrived at the coach house door. Dane pulled out a key ring, selected one of the keys and opened the door. As she entered she heard a buzzer, and he reached behind her and punched a button. "It's awful how one has to have a security system on one's home," she babbled as she preceded him up the stairs. Glancing over her shoulder, she was surprised to see him reset the system. He noticed her watching him, and explained, "We'll go across and look at the paintings in the main house before you leave, if you like. I have some interesting ones done by the Group of Seven and a Harold Towne I am sure will interest you."

By this time they had reached a landing at the top of the stairs and Dane opened the door, inviting her to enter. She found herself in what seemed to be a bachelor apartment. To her left was a large window overlooking the front lawn. Before it was a desk, empty of everything but a brightly ribboned glass paperweight. To her right was a very small kitchen, while before her was an old but comfortable-looking chintz-covered sofa. On the wall opposite her, a picture dominated the room.

There, smiling out at the world, was her mother! And Lynn remembered everything, as one might when one has read partway into a book before a significant action or image triggered one's memory of the book's contents.

Her mother—young, her hair as raven as her own, eyes as blue as hers, and with that exquisite nose that her subconscious mind had chosen because she had always admired it, smiled down at her. She was dressed in a simple white shirt with rolled sleeves and a longish blue denim skirt. Leaning on her lap was her ten-year-old self, smiling into her mother's face and holding up a bunch of wildflowers for her pleasure. She was dressed in a soft blue T-shirt and white shorts, and stood with one bare foot crossed over the other. Her dark hair was divided in braids. One hung down her back while the other one dangled over her shoulder and rested on her mother's lap. She had her father's arrogant nose. She was smiling at her mother with trust and affection as she offered her the flowers.

At the same time that she recognized the picture and those in it, she recognized her mortal enemy, her stepbrother, Dane Copeland. He who had ridiculed her as an adolescent, who had made her years at the university as difficult as possible, and who had tried to murder her!

She was to marvel later just how quickly one could think when one's survival depended on it. Turning to her antagonist, she found that he was watching her with those terrifying eyes and she schooled herself to keep calm. With a great effort, she held herself to the character of Lynn and exclaimed, ''What a lovely young woman. She does look like me, doesn't she? Do you have any idea who she is? I presume that the child is her daughter.''

Looking at him guilelessly, she waited for his answer. He watched her carefully, and then, as if he had come to some kind of decision, he said, ''I believe that the woman is the artist, Martine Hébért, and that the child is her daughter.''

''That's amazing!'' she enthused. ''We have a canvas by the same artist hanging in the house where I live.'' And then she could not help pushing him just a little. ''According to my employer, Adam Stone, Martine Hébért is dead. Is her child alive? I wonder if she inherited her mother's ability.''

Again she looked at him as innocently as she could and waited for a reply. He answered in an indifferent tone, ''The artist died of cancer quite a while ago. I know nothing about the child. The picture itself has skyrocketed in value.'' Liar, she thought.

And then she overplayed her role. Reaching out, she touched the flowers held by the child and commented, ''The flowers look like the same ones that are in the picture in Adam's house. I must tell him.''

Even as she uttered the last words, she sensed him stiffen beside her and glancing up, found his eyes on her wrist. The scars! Dear God, she had forgotten all about the scars. And from the look on his face, she was sure that he was about to make the connection.

Hurriedly, she looked at her watch and made for the door as she said, "Look at the time. I left a note for Adam telling him that I would be back by nine to make breakfast." For a second she thought that she had made it, and then she felt him grab her right arm and swing her around. "Not so fast, my dear. What on earth happened to your wrists?"

Oh, God help me, she prayed. What kind of story will explain them? Assuming as much dignity and indignation as she could muster, she tried to yank her arm away, look embarrassed and mumble, "If you must know, I was depressed and tried to take my life."

He kept his grip on her arm and yanked her toward him. "Tell me another one, Sarah. Let me see your ankles."

That did it. If she didn't get free now, she never would. Frantically, she reached for her beeper and before he realized what she was doing, pulled the pin. The resulting noise nearly did her in and completely disabled him long enough for her to break free of his grasp and head for the door. She had almost reached it again when he managed to lunge forward and catch her ankle. Frantic now, she tried to twist her leg free. As she struggled, she looked around for something to use as a weapon. Her eye fell on the paperweight and she seized it. Before she could aim it at his head, he managed to pull her toward him, and with one final effort, she threw it at the plate-glass window. With the shattering of the glass, an alarm began to peal.

As he threw her to the floor, he screamed above the cascading shrieks of the beeper and the pealing of the security system. "Where's the deed?" He was like one demented, shaking her, banging her head against the floor and finally squeezing the life out of her.

Even as everything began to disappear into blackness, she felt his hands release her. She was vaguely aware of Sam's voice saying, "For heaven's sake, leave him. You'll kill him. Help Lynn. She needs you."

Gasping frantically for breath, she felt Adam's hands on her, touching her face and calling her name. Her vision cleared and she tried to get up, to tell him that she knew who she was, but all she could manage was a rasp of sound. Then Adam was cradling her head against his shoulder, lifting her, and moving her away from danger.

She was never sure whether she really remembered what happened next or just recalled other people's descriptions. As Adam turned to carry her toward the stairs, heavy steps pounded up them, and to her amazement, two police officers entered, guns before them, shouting for everyone to freeze. She heard one of the officers say, "Sam? What's going on here?" and Sam answered with the most welcome words in the language, "Arrest this man for the attempted murder of this young woman. We barely stopped him from choking her to death." And as Adam swung around, she was amazed to see Sam on top of Dane, holding his face down and twisting his arm high above his back.

After that, she sank into shock, still hardly able to breathe and barely aware of the scene around her as Dane Copeland argued ineffectually to be set free and was finally led downstairs, his hands handcuffed behind his back. By now, backup men had arrived and police were everywhere. Sam seemed important in a way that she could not understand, but Adam held her, safe.

As they finally began to move toward the stairs, she realized that they were leaving the painting behind. With an effort, she tried to tell Adam to bring the picture. One of the policeman heard her and said, "Sorry, it belongs to Mr. Copeland. We can't move it."

But she persisted, grabbing the officer's arm and rasping out the words, "The picture is not Dane's. It's mine. My name is Sarah James." She felt Adam stiffen at those words, but continued on, "The woman in the picture is my mother. Legally, all this is mine. Bring the picture. It contains evidence.'

The constable's face was a study in incredulity when he heard her name. "Sarah James, the missing girl?" he asked.

Adam answered for her. "That's right. Bring the picture, but before we go to any police station, I'm taking her over to Sunnybrook to be checked." The officer nodded in agreement and in no time they were down the stairs and in a squad car heading for the hospital. Sarah closed her eyes, relaxed in Adam's arms and knew that she was safe, safe from danger for the first time in four months.

Adam glanced at his watch. It had been thirty minutes since they had whisked Lynn away to be examined. Thirty endless minutes. Minutes in which he had relived the events of the morning over and over again. They made it to the coach house apartment in

time only because Sam had had the foresight to put
Copeland under observation. His operative had jogged
by Copeland when he had been talking to Lynn and
had recognized her. His van had been just beyond
Copeland's house near the ravine, and he had telephoned Sam at Adam's to tell him that Lynn was even
at that moment walking up the driveway to Copeland's
house.

Adam was sure that he never would have found her
in time if it had not been for Sam's cool-headed drive
over the short distance to Copeland's, for he had been
too terrified to think clearly. All the way over, his
mind had been filled with images, each more terrible—Dane discovering who Lynn was, Dane trying
her up again, Dane trying to kill her. Even as they had
leaped from the car, the air had suddenly been rent by
the sound of Lynn's beeper. Seconds later, even as
they headed up the driveway, the window in the coach
house had shattered, and the security system began to
peal. When they reached the door, Sam made short
order of the lock by simply shooting it off and Adam
had taken the stairs three at a time.

A tremor shook his body as he remembered the
scene he encountered. Dane Copeland was kneeling
over Lynn, one hand on her throat. Before his horrified
eyes, he saw him raise his other hand in a fist ready
to smash her head. Even as he sprinted across the
room, he watched Dane's arm complete its arc and
begin to descend. Like a slow-motion movie, he saw
the fist moving closer to her head. He threw himself
through the air and at the last second, knocked him
sideways off her.

Suddenly finding the waiting room claustrophobic,

he stood up and went out into the hall to stare sight-lessly out a window. He was shaken by his actions, by the very violence of them, and by the realization that he would do the same thing again if Lynn was ever in danger. He shuddered as he remembered his rage as he pounded Copeland. For sure he would have killed him if Sam had not hauled him away and yelled, "Help Lynn. She needs you."

Now, he was swept with remorse. How clever he had thought he would be, finding out Lynn's past. He had never really believed that his actions could lead her into such danger. His arrogance and selfishness had nearly killed her. He had had to have her as his own as soon as possible, but with no regard to the consequences. Would she ever forgive him? Could he ever forgive himself?

Ironically, now he had his wish and she did know who she was. But would she want him? Why would she want him? Wouldn't she want to return to her studies, enjoy herself as a bright, beautiful student and capture those experiences that she had never had be-fore?

Adam was sure he had lost her. After all, she had met Dane Copeland and risked going into his house without asking him for assistance. Didn't that indi-cate that she saw her life without him? A hand on his shoulder startled him and he turned to see Tom. His cousin's expression was grave and Adam felt a rush of panic return. "Lynn? Is she going to be all right?"

"Lynn's fine," he said. "She'll be coming out in a few moments. Adam, what on earth happened? She is black and blue with bruises, one rib was nearly rebroken and she came within an inch of having her larynx fractured.''

Briefly Adam described the struggle in the coach house. Tom shook his head in wonderment. ''Lynn says you saved her life.''

''I may have been the one who knocked Dane off her, but Sam was the one with the foresight to set up surveillance. His operative was the one who was quick enough to recognize Lynn and let us know there was a problem,'' Adam stated bitterly. ''I was the one whose schemes put her in danger.''

Tom heard the despair in Adam's voice and hastened to reassure him. ''Then you were right in hiring Sam, weren't you?'' Changing the subject, he said, ''We wanted Lynn to stay in overnight, but she refuses. She wants to go to the police station and get the interviews over right away. I think she is afraid that her stepbrother will somehow manage to get free if she doesn't. I've got some medication here. Give it to her before she rests. All it is is a relaxant to help those neck muscles ease up and to give her a good sleep. Give me a call when you have everything straightened out.'' And with that he turned and walked back through Emergency.

It was not until one o'clock in the afternoon that Lynn and Adam arrived at the police station. When they entered the office of the detective in charge of the Sarah James case, Lynn was surprised to see Sam already present as well as the jogger who had passed Dane and herself in front of the house. In fact, now she remembered that he had also been in the coach house when the police had stormed the place.

Sam stepped forward and pulled a chair out for her before the desk of the detective. Adam sat down on the chair beside her.

The detective was a tall man, similar to Sam in stature, but slightly balding and inclined to heaviness. When Sam introduced her, he stood and reached across his desk, a grin as wide as the ocean splitting an otherwise nondescript face. ''Young lady,'' he said as he pumped her hand, ''I cannot tell you what a pleasure it is to meet you. Sam has filled me in on many aspects of the case while you and Dr. Stone were at the hospital, but now I would like to hear your story. Do you feel able to do this now, or would you rather wait until your throat has healed a little and your voice is stronger?''

All Sarah was able to do was nod and whisper, ''Now.''

Leaning over, the detective turned on a tape recorder, identified the time and those present, and then asked, ''What would you like me to call you, Sarah or Lynn?''

The question took her breath away. She really had not had time to come to grips with the fact that her memory had returned. In the hospital, her initial distress had been over the fact that they insisted Adam leave her while she was examined. There, a variety of medical staff had prodded and questioned her about her condition and the constable had insisted that pictures be taken of her injuries. Just when she had felt that she could bear no more, Tom had come in. That he was shocked by her injuries was evident.

Not one joke, not one teasing remark passed his lips. Instead he quietly checked over her jaw to his satisfaction and told her that he would report her condition to Adam.

Since then, all the way down to the station, her mind had been completely occupied by the fact that Adam was not himself. Although he held her tightly in the police car, he had not spoken more than a dozen words. To make matters worse, he looked terrible. His face was drawn and gray, lines ran tightly from his nose to mouth, and his lips were outlined in white. She began to wonder whether he had been hurt in the struggle to free her, but before she could ask they had reached the station and were led upstairs.

Now this detective wanted to know what she wanted to be called. What he really wanted to know was who she thought she was. Well, there was no way of avoiding the truth. She knew who she was. She was Sarah James. But she was also the Sarah James who had lived as Lynn MacDougall.

She glanced uneasily at Adam, but he was no help. Unconsciously, she fingered her jaw and nose. Then, with a smile that rocked the hardened detective, she answered, "Please call me Sarah."

The detective nodded and continued, "Sam has filled me in on your very fortunate escape from the bus accident in August, and about the resulting amnesia." Surprised, she looked at Sam. How did he know all that? "If you feel up to it, will you fill in the details of your life from the day you left Queen's University last August until the moment of the accident?"

In spite of herself, Lynn felt a curl of nausea roll

through her stomach and a beading of perspiration form on her lip. In a whisper, she rasped out the question, "Is Dane free or behind bars?"

The detective seemed to understand the reason for her question, for he leaned toward her and smiled his reassurance. "Believe me, Sarah, at this moment he is behind bars. There is no way that he can harm you."

However, his assurance was not enough. She pressed on. "Will he get out on bail?"

"That remains to be seen," he replied. "However, now that we have found you alive, we intend to keep you that way. We so rarely have a happy ending in cases like yours that we'll do anything to ensure your safety."

Glancing up at Adam again for assurance, she began: "I had been fortunate enough to receive a teaching position as well as a scholarship from Queen's for this year. For the first time in my life, I was able to afford to live off campus in an apartment of my own. So, on the sixteenth of August, I headed to my stepbrother's coach house to remove my remaining belongings."

"You lived with your stepbrother?" the detective interjected.

"Not exactly," she explained. "In my father's will, he left the coach house apartment for my use while I was still in school. When I completed my education, it was to revert to my stepbrother. However, Dane and I had never seen eye to eye and I could not wait to move away. There was not much of mine in the apartment anyway, just a few textbooks, some clothes, and the painting of my mother."

At this point, she stopped and asked for a drink of water. Anything, she realized, to delay continuing her story. Finally the water was gone, and there was no more avoiding it. Even as she began to talk, she could feel her heart speed up and perspiration break out on her forehead. "I arrived at the apartment at about five o'clock, took up my overnight bag and then went out for some supper. I returned about seven and carted up the cardboard boxes into which I intended to pack my belongings. I figured that I could have it all done by eleven, even have the car packed so that in the morning I could leave for a doctor's appointment and then return to Kingston. You can imagine my consternation when later I saw lights draw up before the coach house and my stepbrother get out of the car.

"There have been many bizarre circumstances since I left Kingston that day. Many of them were fortuitous—having Dr. Dunlop, Adam's cousin, operate on my jaw," and she glanced up at Adam, "and working for Adam. But believe me, on that sixteenth of August, luck was definitely against me when Dane arrived."

The detective leaned forward, smiled encouragingly and asked, "How so?"

She studied the empty glass still clutched in her hand and forced back the urge to ask for more water. Taking a large breath, she continued, "Dane disappeared around to the front of the house and for a few minutes I thought that he was not going to bother me. The next thing I knew, I heard him step into the hall that formed a connecting passage to the main house and then enter the apartment.

"Dane could see that I was packing, and he walked

around the room sticking his nose into the boxes that were full. Finally, he came to the point of his visit. He said that he had some papers that he wanted me to sign, and that I had saved him a trip to Kingston.''

Her throat was on fire and her voice was a mere rasp. "I'm sorry," she whispered, "but do you think that you would have something warm I could drink? My throat really hurts."

Out of the corner of her eye she saw Adam start to stand, but the detective was not about to let her delaying tactics or Adam interfere with the telling of the events. He asked quickly, "What would you like, tea or coffee?"

The thought of some warm, healing tea made her smile and she replied, "Tea, please," unaware that the hardened detective was again dazzled by her smile.

He ordered the tea and then turned back to her, evidently expecting her to continue. With a sigh, she obliged. "I was immediately on guard when he mentioned signing something." She paused, waiting hopefully for the tea to miraculously arrive. When it did not, she had to continue. "I asked him what it was he needed me to sign. He pulled out a sheaf of papers and placed them on the desk. Then he explained to me that he had a chance to make a small fortune for me. All he needed was my cooperation. I have little regard for Dane's integrity in business. My father had at least been honest, if ruthless, when it came to making a dollar, but Dane's projects were always suspect and only ever profited him. So when he mentioned making me a fortune, I almost laughed in his face.

"He proceeded to tell me that he had planned a

condominium complex on the land on which my mother's home stood. The fact that there would be a marina attached to the complex on the St. Lawrence River was a surefired drawing card for the wealthy of the area. Then he turned to me and said, 'We can start as soon as you sign here and hand over the deed for the property.'

"I was stunned that he would have the colossal nerve to try such a scheme. There was no way that he had the legal right to touch the property. The house and land belonged to me, my name was on the deed, and at my mother's instruction the deed was well-hidden. More important, it had been my lifelong dream to restore the house that he had let go to ruin. Now that my doctorate was in sight, I had even made plans to repair it the minute I had saved enough money. Consequently, I said that I would not sign and that I would never give him the deed."

At that moment, the tea arrived and with trembling hands, she held the cup and sipped it while she gathered the courage to go on. Finally she continued. "Dane was furious. He ranted and raged while I continued to tape up boxes and tried to ignore him. Finally, he started to rip them open and shout at me that he would find the deed before he left that night. He frightened me and as he tossed the things from the boxes, I headed for the telephone to phone the police. I am not sure if what happened next would have happened if I had just let him search through the boxes. All I know is that when he realized what I was about to do, he grabbed the telephone from my hand and then twisted my arm behind my back. I remember he kept saying as he inched my arm higher, 'Come on, little stepsister. I need that deed and no court in the land will keep me from getting it. Your father left me the right to make money for you. Where is it?'

"At that, I kicked him but he swung me around and began to shake me. I struggled and slipped, and think that I must have fallen and hit my head on the desk, for I don't remember anything else."

"Nothing?" asked the detective, disappointment obvious in his voice.

Sipping the tea again and resting her voice, she tried to gather the strength to go on with her story. Having just remembered it, it was as fresh as if it had just happened, and she could feel panic tighten her chest. Her voice was high and strained as she explained. "The next thing I remember was waking in a hot, dark, cramped place that smelled of gasoline. I was horrified to discover that my wrists and ankles were tied behind my back and that a heavy, suffocating blanket covered me. It took a few minutes to realize that I must be in the trunk of some kind of vehicle because I was constantly being jostled and could hear the sounds of traffic; however, whatever I was in seemed to be riding on something as it swayed sideways rather than bumping along as a car would on a road."

She stopped and had to put the cup down as her hand was trembling violently. This time her distress was so obvious that even the hardened detective had no heart to make her continue. He said gently, "Would you like to take a break or continue in the morning?"

But the thought of Dane somehow managing to get

out on bail if the evidence was not clear made her pull herself together. Shaking her head, she hurried on. "After a while, my panic subsided and I realized that Dane, true to form, had taken the moment offered to him and turned it to his advantage. After all, it was unlikely anyone had seen him arrive. His house is too private for that. And anyway, it had been a thoroughly unpleasant evening, with winds and heavy rain. It did not take me many minutes to figure out that Dane intended to get rid of me. That caused another period of panic. I struggled with the binding on my ankles and wrists, but only managed to tighten them. Then I remembered. I was wearing a pair of cotton trousers with pockets on the outside of the legs, down by my calves. In one of the pockets, I carried my credit card, a hundred dollar bill and a nail file. I only carried my driver's license, a bit of cash and a paperback in my handbag," she explained.

She stopped and grinned. "Dane made one fatal error. He did not check the pockets on my trouser legs. With a great deal of effort, I was able to get my hand under the buttoned flap and pull out the nail file. After that, it was a piece of cake, although," she said ruefully and showed the detective her wrists, "I managed to scar both ankles and wrists. Dane had used plastic fish line, and although it would not break when I tried to pull on it, it filed apart easily."

Again, she rested her voice and had some tea. Having got through the part where she gained consciousness in the car trunk, she felt much better and carried on with the story.

"When I was free, I explored the trunk with my hands and realized that I was in my own little car.

Again, this was to my advantage because I knew that under the spare tire there was a loose tire rod. I managed to get it and then covered myself up with the blanket again and waited. Oh yes, I did two other things. I made sure that my bleeding wrists came in contact with as much of the trunk as I could manage, and I pulled out several pieces of hair and hooked them up into the fretwork of the trunk lid. Did you find them?''

The detective smiled and assured her that they had. He explained that they had assumed the worst when they discovered the blood and hair. Then he said, ''Obviously, you escaped. Would you tell us how?''

It was easier to describe what happened next than to recount her experiences in the car trunk. ''Dane took me somewhere up north of Kaladar off Highway Seven. He drove deep into the forest along an old loggers' road and stopped near a very high, rocky cliff overlooking a lake. When he opened the trunk of the car and lifted me out, I hit him with the tire rod and ran for my life. I stumbled among rocks and trees; my progress made doubly dangerous now as the rain had stopped and the moon kept shining from behind fast-moving clouds.'' Turning to Adam, she explained, ''That must have been what I was dreaming about in my nightmares. That and being tied up in the car trunk.''

Adam had sat beside her silently since their arrival. He still looked terrible and only nodded at her explanation. The detective kept her on track. ''Didn't your stepbrother chase you?''

''Yes, he did. He drove me toward the edge of the

cliff but before he caught up, I slipped and fell over. I saved myself by grabbing some bushes that grew out of the rock and managed to get my footing on a narrow ledge. Then, I was able to slip beneath a granite overhang. I could hear Dane moving about, could see the beam of his flashlight and was afraid that he would follow me down. I had a cotton shirt on over my T-shirt and so I removed it, tied up a stone in it, threw it into the water below and, at the same time, shoved a pile of dirt off the ledge into the lake. When Dane spotted the shirt in the beam of his flashlight, all that remained of the shirt was a slight billowing of cotton. It disappeared as he watched. In spite of that he waited for what seemed hours. Finally, near dawn, he drove away.

"I stayed there for the entire day, huddled on the ledge of that granite cliff." Turning to Adam, she said, "It was pink granite, like the house. Ironic, isn't it? No wonder I always felt safe there. Only in the early evening did I have the courage to venture forth. I followed the loggers' road out to the county road leading down to Highway Seven. Tired, I sat down and wondered how I was going to get away from there when a pickup approached. Another lucky coincidence. The truck developed a flat tire and the two men who were in it had to stop and change it. I could tell from their conversation that they were going into Kaladar to meet the late-night Ottawa–Toronto bus. As they started up, I ran across and managed to get into the back of the pickup unnoticed. When we reached Kaladar, I waited until they went into the restaurant to get a beer and then slipped out. The restaurant was also the bus stop and

I was able to buy a ticket to Toronto. The bus came almost immediately and I boarded it.''

Sam spoke up from the back. ''I'm curious, Lynn, sorry, I mean Sarah. Why didn't you call the police right then?''

''Sheer, unmitigated terror. I had only one desire and that was to put myself into a position where I was completely surrounded by people. What could have been safer than a bus?'' And then, as she realized the irony of her statement, she began to tremble.

At that, Adam acted. He put his arm around her, and said to the detective, ''I think that we should stop.'' But she was so nearly finished that she shook her head and continued.

''I sat beside a young woman my age. We had a long trip, and soon we were talking together the way one does when one knows that neither will see the other again. Her name was Lynn MacDougall. She told me all about changing her job. She was excited over the fact that she was going to a Blue Jays' game the next day.'' At that, her voice wavered and Adam tightened his grip on her shoulder. ''She was really excited about this. When we got as far as Whitby, we both decided that we should freshen up. She suggested that I go first as she had been traveling in jeans and a T-shirt and wanted to change her clothes because she had treated herself to a room in the hotel at the SkyDome. When I returned, she got out into the aisle. At the last moment, she asked me to hold her purse. I thought she was crazy to let a stranger do this; however, she explained that she did not have room for it in the small washroom if she took her small suitcase. To please her, I agreed, and put the purse strap over my head. I remember holding on to it tightly as I went to slip into my seat.''

Then her voice really quavered, and in her distress she was unable to stop the flow of tears. She whispered, ''I don't remember anything else but I know she must have been the person who died in the accident. She would have been alive had she not been so considerate and let me go first.''

''That's it,'' Adam declared. ''If you want anything more, come out to the house tomorrow.''

The detective realized that both Sarah and the grim-faced man beside her had reached their limit so he agreed, and arranged to have them taken home in a police cruiser. When Adam questioned the need for a cruiser and suggested a taxi, the detective said wryly, ''If I know the various crime reporters that haunt our halls for a story, they will have already caught wind of a break in Sarah's case. Since they have no idea where she lives, the least we can do is sneak the pair of you out and take you home. Anyway, I was just told, when I phoned for the cruiser, that the winter storm forecast has arrived earlier than expected. You would find it hard to get a taxi.''

As they waited the detective said, ''Just two fast questions, Sarah. What did you intend to do when you got to Toronto and why is this painting so important?''

By now, both Sarah and Adam were standing. However, she stopped and answered his questions. ''I intended to go right to the police station. The painting is important because the deed to the St. Lawrence property and my will are hidden in the picture frame. My mother made the frame herself. Artists do that to save money. She showed me how to take it apart and slip folded papers in it so that no one was the wiser.''

To Adam's annoyance, the detective persisted. ''Where is the will hidden?''

Anxious to get it all over, Sarah walked to the frame and pointed to a series of small screws on each of the corners. ''Unscrew these, and the first layer of the frame will detach itself. In the space between the two parts, you'll find the papers.''

To her surprise, the detective rooted around in his desk drawer and then walked around with a small set of screwdrivers. ''I always knew that I would use these some day,'' he grinned. Kneeling down before the back of the picture, he carefully unscrewed the outside part of the frame. When he lifted it off, the papers fell to the ground. With a smile, he held up one deed and one will. ''We have him now, Sarah, not only on attempted murder but also on fraud. You need never worry about him bothering you again!''

When they arrived at the house, Adam stopped the two officers from taking the car into the driveway. He saw no point in their getting snarled in the drifts that were beginning to form across it. When the officers expressed concern about completing their assignment and delivering Sarah right to the door, Adam assured them that he would carry her, and so he did.

Jumping out of the cruiser, Adam leaned in and picked Sarah up. The gale hit them immediately, and she clung tightly to him, hiding her face against his neck as he battled the wind and snow up the short drive to the doorway. Swiftly he unlocked the door while still holding her, then hurried in, followed by a flurry of snowflakes. Slamming the door with his foot, he turned toward the security system and Sarah reached out and punched in the numbers. Laughing, she brushed the snow from Adam's face where it clung to his hair and sat on his eyelashes. He laughed and blew at the flakes that had settled on her hair. Then, again, she felt him withdraw. He slipped off his sodden running shoes and headed down the stairs and across the living room toward her room, but she objected. "I want to go to the solarium," she rasped out.

In the end, they compromised. Sarah had a shower, changed into another warm track suit, and dragged her duvet and pillow with her to the solarium while Adam changed, made soup, shared it with her and supervised the pill-taking. Even then, Sarah had to put her foot down. "I will only take half a pill because as soon as I have rested and my throat feels better, we are going to have a serious talk."

Sarah woke slowly. Short, episodic patches of dreams floated through her consciousness. She remembered the terrible day that her mother had told her she was ill and would die. Then she remembered her mother painting the picture for her. She remembered her mother saying that while Sarah had the picture to look at, she would never feel alone. She would always be reminded that her mother loved her and would continue to love her long after she was gone.

And it had been true. Sarah had gone to the picture whenever her life had been lonely; whenever her father was about to send her off to yet another summer camp, or whenever Dane had ridiculed her disappearing chin.

Sarah remembered another moment with her mother that she had not thought of in years. Had she dreamed it or was it just that memory had chosen to bring forth the incident now?

Sarah's mother had tried to explain what happened between her father and herself that caused their marriage to end even before Sarah's birth. "We each thought the other was something other than we were. I thought that he would stay with me in Kingston, work at his career here, and rejoice in my success. He thought that my painting was just a hobby and that I would give it all up and become the perfect society wife. Why we never discussed these things before we married I will never know. We were so in love that it never entered our minds that we had no attitudes or goals in common.

"In the end, your father thought that I had trapped him and he left with a great sense of bitterness. I am afraid that you will find that bitterness will also be applied to you."

Then Sarah remembered that her mother had cupped Sarah's face in her hands and said, "Sarah. Someday, you will fall in love. When you do, be sure that it is the whole person that you see and care for. Make sure that you understand those things that interest your partner and be sure that you can share his pleasure in them. Make sure that he also understands your needs so that you can enjoy a rich life together. Remember this. There are no Prince Charmings to sweep you off your feet. Only ordinary men who will have as many flaws as you have."

Her mother had lifted her on to her knee and held her closely while she stroked her hair and rocked her. Softly, she had whispered, "If you are lucky enough to find such a person, then risk everything to win him and share your life with him. But do not settle for less. Do not settle for someone who wants you to be less than your best!"

The images of her dream drifted away to be replaced by the sound of the blizzard outside. Opening her eyes, she realized the Christmas tree lights were off and she could see the raging storm in all its frightening violence. In the eerie light of the city, the trees at the back of the yard tossed and bent in the gale. Clouds of snow were picked up, swirled around in the yard and thrown against the glass. The shrubs before the windows thrashed against the panes in a frenzy.

She lay with her face on her hand, watching the frantic scene, thankful that she was safe inside. A soft sound on the other side of the Christmas tree caught her attention. Looking closely, she realized that Adam was standing before the glass, obviously as fascinated with the storm as she had been. For a while, she lay there watching his silhouette; his head, his long lithe body, the line of his shoulders, the rise and fall of his breathing. It came to her that her mother was right. If she loved Adam, then she must continue to take risks just as she had that morning when she ran into Dane.

Moving quietly, she got up and tiptoed over to the switch that turned on the Christmas tree lights. Even as he turned at the sound of her movement, the lights bathed the room in a low, warm glow. Before he could speak, she was beside him. Adam looked down at her and she saw pain and suffering in his face.

She reached out and touched his arm. She felt him tense beneath her fingers and try to move away, but she would have no part of this. "Adam, what is the matter?" she whispered.

He looked down at her for the longest time and finally reached out a hand and gently cupped her chin. Then he completely startled her by asking, "Can you ever forgive me?"

Sarah shook her head in confusion. "Forgive you for what?"

"For putting your life in danger."

Sarah was still unable to figure out what he was talking about. "Danger? When did you ever do that? For goodness sake, Adam, you saved my life today. One second later and I am sure that Dane would have killed me."

But Adam was shaking his head, a look of such anguish on his face that Sarah could only stare and wait for whatever explanation he would give.

"Don't you understand, Sarah, I had to have my own way. I wanted you to remember your past. I knew that you would never let yourself care for me while your memory was lost." He turned away from her and stared out the window. Then he went on, "I was the one who arranged that you come with me to the party and the theater. I was the one who thought that I could handle any situation that might arise. In my arrogance and selfishness, I put your life at risk. It is something that I can never forgive myself for."

Sarah heard those words with her heart rather than her head. Adam cared for her. That meant that Adam must love her. She nearly threw herself in his arms before she thought about Adam's words, but the pain in his voice stopped her. Adam really felt that he had endangered her, she realized.

She touched his arm again and finally reached for his other arm and turned him around to face her. "Adam. If you had waited until I had the courage to discover who I was, nothing would have happened. I would never have had the nerve to go to the shopping center, let alone to a party. Without your actions, I would still be less than a person. Because of you, I am whole."

And then drawing upon all the courage she could muster, she reached up and touched his cheek. "Adam. Now I know who I am, and I know that I love you with all my heart."

She felt a tremor run through him as she said those words and yet he held back. She repeated herself. "Adam. I love you."

Finally, the words burst out of him. "If you loved me, why did you go to see Dane all by yourself? If you remembered who you were, why didn't you ask me to help you?"

Then she understood. He felt betrayed. She realized that in spite of all the talking that had occurred in the detective's office, there were facts that had not been clarified. She could not stop the smile of joy that crossed her face as she began to explain away the last of the obstacles between them. "Adam. When I met Dane on the street, I thought it was just a piece of good fortune. I had already decided last night after you fell asleep in my arms that I was going to discover my past. The first step was to ask you to go with me to see Dane's picture.''

"I could not believe my eyes when I ran into him this morning. To be honest, he frightened me, but I couldn't say why. I certainly did not feel safe with him. But then, I thought to myself, this is a risk worth taking. If I find out something about myself, then just possibly this new knowledge might solve my identity and I will know whether I am free to love you.

"I went with Dane because I loved you. It was only when I saw my mother's picture that I remembered everything. Then I wished with every fiber of my being that you were with me because I knew that I was in danger.''

At those words, Adam gathered her into his arms and held her tightly, as if he was afraid that she would disappear. He buried his face in her hair and whispered, "Oh, my love . . . '' Then he was covering her face with kisses and between kisses, saying, "As long as I live, I will never forget those moments after Sam's operative telephoned and said that he had seen you accompanying Dane into his house. I will never forget hearing your beeper start to sound as we arrived at the house or the moment I saw Dane about to smash your head in.'' Holding her face between trembling hands, he whispered, "I thought I had lost you forever.''

Smiling into his face, she said, "Instead, you have me forever.'' After a pause, Sarah asked, "Who *is* Sam Bowers?''

Grinning broadly, Adam put his arm around her and led her to the chesterfield. "You were right. We have to talk.'' And pulling her down into his arms, he explained. They planned and loved far into the night, while outside the storm continued to rage . . .

It was Christmas Eve. Adam stood before the communion table in the old Gothic church where he and Tom had sung as children. To his left and right were the richly carved choir stalls, now dimmed to shadows by flickering candelabras. In these sat family and friends, waiting with him for his bride to appear around the corner of the pulpit. Off in the distance at the back of the church the choir sang a joyful ''Gloria'' beneath an illuminated rose window.

For the umpteenth time in the last ten days, Adam counted his blessings. His beloved Sarah-Lynn was whole and safe, and in a moment would join him. Because of a generous-minded choir and minister who had given up their time on such a busy evening, they were to be wed in the presence of his parents who had flown in from Japan, his cousin and his family, Alain and his fiancée, Lisette, and Sam Bowers.

The choir finished their singing, and the organ began Sarah's music. Before him, in the soft light of the candles, young Anne, dressed in red velvet, came up the stairs followed by Sarah, holding tightly to Tom's arm. She was resplendent in silk and lace, and on her face was a smile so brilliant that all who witnessed the service claimed that they had never seen a more radiant bride. Adam, taking her hand, trembled with the thought that he had been given far more than any man deserved. As they knelt before the minister, he promised to be worthy of such largesse.

And Sarah knew, as she exchanged her vows with

Adam, that she was blessed, for not only was she gaining a husband whom she loved and honored, but also a family—parents, cousins, a niece and nephew. As the service ended, Adam held her face between his hands and kissed her gently. The choir began to sing "Joy to the World," and it seemed to both of them that indeed, they sang with the angels.